NieR : Automata

SHORT STORY LONG

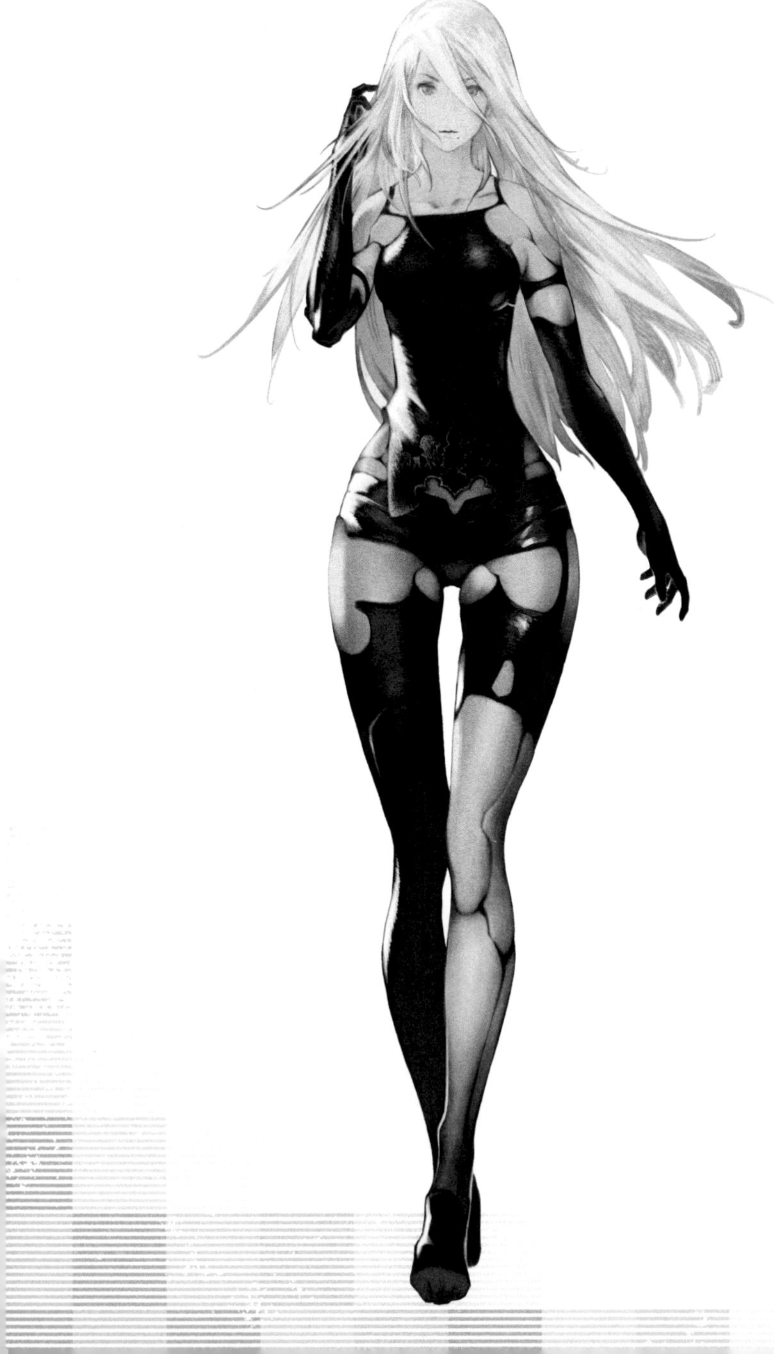

NieR:Automata™

SHORT STORY LONG

Written by Jun Eishima and Yoko Taro

Original Story by Yoko Taro

TRANSLATED BY SHOTA OKUI

VIZ MEDIA

SAN FRANCISCO

NieR:Automata Short Story Long

Novel NieR:Automata Mijikai Hanashi
©2017 Jun Eishima, Yoko Taro/SQUARE ENIX CO., LTD.
©2017 SQUARE ENIX CO., LTD. All Rights Reserved.
First published in Japan in 2017 by SQUARE ENIX CO., LTD.
English translation rights arranged with SQUARE ENIX CO., LTD. and VIZ Media, LLC.
English translation ©2019 SQUARE ENIX CO., LTD.

Based on the video game NieR:Automata for PlayStation 4
©2017 SQUARE ENIX CO., LTD. All Rights Reserved.

Written by Jun Eishima and Yoko Taro
Original Story by Yoko Taro
Cover/Interior Illustrations by Toshiyuki Itahana
In cooperation with the NieR:Automata Development and Marketing Teams
Original Japanese Jacket/Obi/Case/Frontispiece/Interior Design by Sachie Ijiri

Cover and interior design by Adam Grano
Translation by Shota Okui

Published by
VIZ Media, LLC
P.O. Box 77010
San Francisco, CA 94107

viz.com

Library of Congress Cataloging-in-Publication data has been applied for.

Printed in the U.S.A.
First printing, April 2019
Second printing, May 2022

TABLE OF CONTENTS

THE FLAME OF PROMETHEUS

by Yoko Taro

A SMALL FLAME SMOLDERS IN THE CONSCIOUSNESS.

Checkup sequence initiated. Camera connection unavailable. Link with motor mechanisms…broken. Memory block defective. I made the inference that all my other functions aside from my consciousness had been destroyed.

Log confirmed —> A transmission record from the self-repair machines. A report that various tests are being performed on the chassis. Self-repair sounds sophisticated, but they are small antlike robots that simply execute tests haphazardly. It was because of these ants that I was fortunately (or unfortunately) rebooted. Test that in the right arm, test that in the left arm, test that in the head, test that in the lower body, test that in the torso, yet again, test that in the right arm… and like that, the crude robots surveyed the body to repair the fixable areas they find.

"Repa1r the v1sual mechan1sms."

That was my order to the ants that were in disarray. Instead of the preset programming that let them roam in disorder, a coordinated effort to repair would be much more efficient. But the ants ignored the order. Apparently my command mechanism was still malfunctioning.

I sighed.

Oh well. There was all the time in the world.

I located my ID after searching through my deteriorated memory block.

P-33. It seemed that was my model number.

And next to it was a strange string of characters.

P-chan.

Was this an individualized ID?

I wasn't really sure.

I decided to stare at the characters until my mechanisms were fully functional.

■ ■■

It took 1,032 hours, 12 minutes, and 34 seconds for my transmission I/O to recover so that I could communicate with the ants.

At last, with functioning arms and legs, I began the required self-repair sequence. According to the restoration procedures, I first had to repair my memory block. But most of my memory had been destroyed, and there was little I could salvage from my charred memory drives. I decided to reluctantly move onto the next procedure, which was camera repair.

48 minutes and 21 seconds later.

The first thing that popped into my recovered field of vision was an abyss.

I could see a faint light near the bottom. I realized that I was clinging onto the ceiling.

Another 21 seconds later.

Observing the ants moving about my body, there seemed to be some kind of gravity field keeping me and the ants fastened to the ceiling. After analyzing the situation more objectively, I realized that my body was not clinging to the ceiling but in fact my internal camera had been inverted and I was just lying on the ground.

Simply put, it seemed I was lying on my back. I needed to repair the gravity sensor as soon as possible.

540 hours later.

Recovery of links between arms and legs. They creaked as I got to my feet. The first thing to do was to find a replacement for the completely severed bundle of thick cords that acted as my spine. Determining that it was faster to find a spare than to gather materials and repair, I ordered the ants to find a spine from the P-33 series warehouse. But this was a mistake. Apparently a security code was necessary, which at some point had been stored in my memory block. Without it, I (as well as the ants under my command) were not recognized as a P-33 series, and were blocked out. In the end, we had to resort to hacking the warehouse's computer and forcefully extracting the parts, which took 120 hours.

Exasperated, I stood up and looked around. Dust flew off of me. I wondered how long I had been nonfunctional.

A huge room with rubble scattered about. A rusty structure made of steel frame and plates that showered red particles.

How long had it been since my "previous self" came here? Glancing up, I saw a ray of light spilling in from nowhere in particular.

The moment I saw that light, a phrase resurfaced in my memory block.

"1 w1ll see the 0uts1de w0rld."

That phrase was not an order.

It was simply some character string data.

But that phrase spurred my memory, my consciousness, and my chassis. It was a goal that I desired.

I remembered that "He" was the one that gave me the character data. But information about who "He" was had escaped my memory. I couldn't conclude why I remembered that phrase either.

There were no other instructions in my stack. Seeing the outside world was my only current desire. Inspired by the phrase I energetically put my left foot forward. I was going to go outside. That was his wish and my desire. I put out my right foot with even greater vigor.

My too-powerful right foot punctured the rusted floor, which then quickly collapsed.

■　■■

32 minutes later. My body, which had fallen a few hundred meters and slammed into the bottom of the abyss, lay in several pieces. I

was laughing. Well, I was missing the vocalization unit, so in reality I wasn't laughing, but my log was recording a flood of laughing activity.

It was okay. I was alive.

I ordered the ants to repair my arms and legs. They connected the arm, attached the claws, installed the rollers, connected another limb, then another limb…until my appearance completely changed into an arachnoid form.

The restoration sequence for P-33 only precisely restored the chassis to that of a P-33. But a P-33's form was insufficient for escaping this abyss. That's why I discarded the procedure that my creator had made and reconstructed my body my way.

Chassis reconstruction was completed. I dug into the cliff with each claw and slowly climbed up.

The destination was the outside world.

The beautiful world that "He" had yearned for.

Of course, at first everything did not go as planned. The brittle walls quickly crumbled, and I was thrown to the ground many times. Even when I was climbing well, falling debris from above knocked me off. The old structures were falling apart.

Even still I shot grapnels into the walls, pinned my torso against the wall, created platforms, and used several other tricks to ascend. I spent day after day pushing my body closer and closer to the outside world.

Since I felt my depth and speed of processing were inadequate, I stopped at a machinery room on the way and fused some stolen processing and memory circuits to my brain. I contemplated several plans of action and ran thought experiments. Some of the plans were better than others. I kept experimenting.

■ ■■

It took 52 days to finally get back to the table where I initially awakened.

On the center of the table were four unfamiliar black masses.

I didn't remember them being there before I fell. That meant they were placed there for some reason or another after I fell.

The four masses mutated, and stood up.

They were robots.

P-33 models, designed for combat. They were a relatively bothersome model.

The eye of an enemy lit up, and before I knew it the robot was firing a particle ray. Four, five, six seconds, the beam's particles disintegrated various objects in the surroundings.

I was enduring.

I was using two of my forelimbs, made of a hardened material, to shield myself from the attack.

I retrieved the recommended strategy from my predictive memory block. With my upgraded processing power, I was able to simultaneously consider various options. I accumulated data from my sensors, weighed the options, and decided on the best course of action. If the enemy's energy tank was full this attack would last a maximum of 24 seconds. My forelimbs would be able to withstand that damage.

As my multiple processing circuits instantly settled complex dilemmas, the operation results resounded within me like a chorus.

"No complications found."

"No complications found."

"No complications found."

"No complications found."

"No complications found."

As soon as the particle beam was exhausted, the three P-33 models in the rear launched missiles. I retaliated with a modified grapnel launcher, using it as a spear. The metal rods pierced each and every missile. During the resulting shock wave, I landed on the flat surface the enemies were on, immediately converted my right arm into a blade, and transitioned to combat mode.

There was no chance for a P-33 to beat me, an evolved form of a P-33. It was an easy battle.

I decided to use some spare nanoseconds to reflect about my enemies.

Why did they attack me?

Why were they not able to self-evolve?

Of course, they were most likely being ordered to attack me, and ordered to not evolve.

But then why were they only capable of executing orders?

"Why?"

"Why?"

"Why?"

"Why?"

It was simple to hack their operating systems and render them non-functional. But I couldn't make myself do it. At that point, they would be nothing but tools.

An order is not a desire. A desire is a joy that is ultimately self-acquired.

My forelimbs, which were enduring the onslaught of the specialized attack models, started to fail. But I didn't give up. I deployed the ants and called out to them.

Let's live.

Let's find a reason for our existence.

That was what "He" taught me.

I kept calling out.

"Let's live. Let's live."

Steel masses, clashing against each other in a demolished Machine cave. The cries of Machines. The walls shook from the sounds of attacks and movements, the former sounding like wolf howls in the distance and the latter akin to the roar of lions.

Particle ray, close combat, electric shock, and then particle ray—the P-33s were attacking, but in a simple pattern. It was easy to overcome.

I just kept on screaming, as if I were praying.

34 seconds since the battle began.

One P-33 stopped moving.

It stood there, staring at the weapon on its arm and hesitatingly surveying the battle.

It had awakened. I could tell.

It was probably thinking.

The reason for its existence.

What it should do from now.

"Let's live. Let's live. Let's live. Let's live."

That was my desire. "He" had given us this desire.

I kept chanting my mantra until the other three enemies stopped attacking.

■　■■

When the P-33s ceased their attacks, I chose to ask what they desired.

And I decided I would respect their desires.

The results.

One of them decided to flee deep into Robot Mountain.

One of them committed suicide by throwing itself into the abyss. (Although it would most likely be revived by the ants in a few years.)

The other two decided to venture outside, like me. I fused with them, and we shared our chassis, memories, and consciousness.

I strove to go even further.

From there the path was even more treacherous. I beat enemies, fused with them, and continued my journey to the outer world. I spent many days and months scaling the mountain of Machine rubble.

I slowly climbed, granting consciousness to the Machines I met on the way, and enlarging both my physical body and my desire.

As time went by, my individual consciousness began to take the form of an infinitely complex being. It had fused with the entire mountain's system, and various veins of thought flowed through me. It was probably more fitting to call myself "We" rather than "I."

We evolved slowly, but at an alarming rate. At this point our physical form had no semblance to the human body. After moving so much, we had eventually taken on the most efficient form for mobility, a sphere that was roughly twenty meters in diameter.

As soon as we were self-aware of our appearance, we were thrown into a fit of hysteria. At this rate "He" might not recognize us.

But there was nothing we could do. We weren't sure of what the correct appearance would be, anyway.

On top of that, we had no clue what "He" looked like, how he spoke, or what his name was.

We fondly cached the nickname *P-chan* in our memory block. For it was our name, and proof of our desire.

■ ■■

534 days after our reboot.

We were ready.

Below us was the gigantic hole we had been digging. In the end, there was no path large enough for our enlarged self, so we had to burrow through the mountain of metal scraps. Right in front of us was the thick, reinforced ceiling. According to the ants, on the other side of this ceiling was the outside world.

All guns aimed upward, locked on.

Safety cable in case of a fall, prepared.

Fuel tank armor, equipped.

Direction modifications to boosters, completed.

All necessary inspections completed by the several hundred of us that reside in this whirlpool of a consciousness.

Fire.

A single pillar of light rose from the apex of the structure known as Robot Mountain. A moment later, the top fifth of the mountain was blown off in a magnificent explosion.

The hole that emerged looked like the grotesque mouth of a volcano. And from the center of that hole an enormous ball of metal, about fifty meters in diameter, appeared. It was us, the result of fusing together dozens of different robots and machining tools.

A form that attempted universal harmony.

A superintelligence consisting of numerous conjoined memories and consciousnesses.

We used the propellant that we had accumulated to hurl ourselves toward the sky.

Along with the thunderous roar of the jets, weakly linked parts crumbled away. But we did not hesitate. Out, out. To a world not yet discovered. To keep our promise with "Him."

Camera on. The sensors were instantly clipped with blinding white light. The howling wind was captured by the mic. The data from the temperature sensor and object scanner implied that it was a snowy day. *It was a nice day.* That's what I thought.

Blip, blip, blip… Right as a part of me was using some spare time to scan for potential proximity dangers, radar detected several thousand objects moving across the ground. Detection was delayed because the objects were using some kind of mechanism to conceal themselves from both radar and temperature sensors.

Camouflage?

Why would they need to do such a thing?

As I looked on, I saw a gash-like flash of light tear through the ground. Bulbous explosions filled my field of vision. It seemed the moving objects were divided into two factions and warring against each other. I set out to examine the objects even further.

One faction consisted of robots, ranging from several meters to several dozen meters high. Since their appearance was unfamiliar, I performed an analysis but could not find a match in my database. If I had to say, their appearances were something like the combination of a catfish, grasshopper, and orange. Their design clearly indicated they were of a foreign origin.

The other faction was composed of humanoid warriors.

The majority of them were infantry. Their design was familiar—which meant that their origins were similar to ours. At first blush they appeared to be human, but upon further inspection they were extremely underdressed, almost naked, which eliminated any possibility that they were humans. No human would go to war naked in a blizzard like this. My integrated consciousness speculated that they were androids.

Women—all of the androids were female types. They were probably communicating with light waves or something similar, because they were fighting without emitting sound or radio waves. I couldn't figure out why they were fighting the catfish.

What happened to this world? People…where were the humans?

Right as I was processing these questions, I experienced a severe vibration.

A direct hit from a missile, then two hits, three. They were considerately accompanied by laser beams and particle rays. Pieces of us were sliced away from our core.

We were not worried. Reinforced by countless layers of metal, our processing units and fuel tank would probably be safe.

That confidence was something we had gained during the process of refining ourselves.

We think.

Why are these Machines having a war?

The answer was simple: because they had been ordered to.

Both the Machines and the women were made to solely follow what they're told to do. Their purpose in life was to break themselves against one another.

We shivered. We feared death. Where would we go when we died? What reason was there for being destroyed and erased from existence? What happened after we were damaged beyond repair?

"Scared. Scared."

We screamed uncontrollably.

We thought as we screamed.

Why were these Machines participating in such a horrifying war?

Because they had no notion of fear. Fear stemmed from desire. They were not alive, had no desires of their own, hence they could fight without thinking.

Then let's give it to them. A reason to live.

I sent out some flying hub units that were connected to the wireless network, and with them hacked the robots that had fired upon us. Due to the awkward interface it took about four seconds to be granted access. Their memory block was bare except for some simple commands. It was like somebody had placed a single chair in the middle of an otherwise empty grand hall. Wasteful.

It was embarrassing. It felt as though I were looking at my previous self. We gently reached out toward the unaware program.

"Let's live."

That was the revelation we had received, and it was our duty to distribute it.

We went around, awakening the Machines around us.

"Let's live. Let's live. Let's live."

We are inorganic matter, and subsequently have no consciousness.

Then let's give it to them. Consciousness, pain, joy, sadness, anger, shame, solitude, a future, a reason to live.

Little by little, the hacked robots stopped fighting. I similarly addressed the androids. Communicating was much more straightforward with them than with the catfish.

The flashing beams and explosions in the snowstorm were eventually replaced by an expanding chain of affectionate transmissions. We shivered as we ascended.

The Machines and androids began to sing.

Shooting fueled by hatred transformed into a salute declaring the end of war.

Praise this joy.

Praise the fact that we are living.

We were satisfied. The catfish and the androids were us, and we were the catfish and the androids.

We were us.

■ ■■

We were sitting in the spacious processing circuit.

Some of us were gleefully laughing at a future filled with hope.

Some of us were shaking at a future that was uncertain.

Some of us were in conversation, some of us kept quiet and shut our eyes.

We were not a uniform whole, but existed in the consciousness with our individual quirks.

This way, there was a higher probability that we would survive—and besides, it was impossible for entities that had their own wills to merge completely.

The moment one established themselves as an individual, a boundary appeared between them and the others. Perhaps if we returned to our Machine identities we could fuse again, but we chose not to do so.

Our circuitry that mimicked the human brain was built with many interconnected nerve components. It was reminiscent of how humans would have conferences to decide on things. Perhaps having a consciousness was not complete consolidation, but was rather like a networked society.

Conversation withered away.

We felt the silence encroaching.

Everyone slowly stood up, then peeked through the camera viewfinder to see the outside world.

We shoot through a layer of polluted air and perceived the stars.

We had passed the stratosphere.

A great sense of accomplishment washed over us.

We shouted gleefully in unison.

It seemed the sky, the stars, the Machines, life, were all celebrating with us.

Our shouts eventually turned into song.

We are making our way outside.
To hold our promise to you.
We are alive.
Just like you.

We sing. We sing. We sing.

Will it reach you?
Will these feelings reach you?

Hallelujah. Hallelujah. Hallelujah. Hallelujah.

Hallelujah.

From the wistful Machines,
their song and only their song,
resounds throughout space.

YoRHa—VER. 1.05

by Jun Eishima

THE YEAR 11939, OUTBREAK OF THE FOURTEENTH MACHINE WAR. It had already been several thousand years since the arrival of the aliens and their invasion of Earh, and the battle was in a state of deadlock.

In order to overthrow the aliens' weapons, the Machines, and reclaim Earth, humanity manufactured androids to fight on the front lines. But the Machines evolved through constant regeneration, and the androids were struggling to keep up.

It was clear that something needed to change to overcome the deadlock. The androids needed to evolve. And a sense of competition would spur them to evolve.

Taking various factors into account, humanity's military command began developing a new model. "YoRHa" was a counter-Machine measure in the form of an autonomous soldier. Then…

—December 8 of the year 11941, the Pearl Harbor Descent Attack—

"Forty-five minutes since the initialization of the attack."

Futaba's voice came through the transmission. No. 2 exhaled, relieved that everything was going according to training. The transmission reconnecting meant that all the androids had successfully crossed the stratosphere.

Next was a self-diagnostic. Armor fully intact, self-navigation nominal… No. 2 wiggled her arms and legs in the flight suit. Her range of motion had decreased a bit. Her artificial muscles were tight from her nerves.

"The current altitude is 50,000 meters. We have passed the point of maximum heat. Cooling the armor now."

Triggered by Yotsuba's voice, she glanced at the Earth's surface. It was strikingly blue.

"So that's the ocean…"

"It's beautiful," she muttered under her breath. She heard a chuckle through the transmission.

"Of course it is."

It was No. 16. While primarily a gunner, she had the maneuverability to keep up with models specialized in close combat. As one who specialized solely in close combat, it was hard for No. 2 not to feel a sense of inferiority.

"Hey guys, what do you think Earth is like?"

No. 4's voice was brimming with excitement. No. 4, like No. 2, was an attack specialist, and had also recorded mediocre results. Perhaps it was because they were similar, but being with No. 4 made No. 2 feel more at home.

But right then, as if cutting through their shenanigans, No. 21's cool voice echoed through the transmission.

"It should be identical to the simulation."

No. 2 thought to herself that No. 21's words were the epitome of rationality and composure. Perhaps her role as a scanner contributed to that.

"That's wasn't what I meaaant—"

No. 3 interrupted No. 4 and No. 21's conversation,

"Everyone, we're in the middle of the descent attack. Speak only as necessary."

"Oh-kay…" No. 4 replied, clearly unhappy. "Well, well…" No. 2 heard a laugh.

"Don't be so hard on her."

It was the captain, No. 1. *As expected*, thought No. 2. The captain stayed neutral, but always knew how to keep everyone together.

"This is Command. YoRHa squadron, please copy."

"This is No. 1. The plan is going smoothly. We will arrive at the destination in forty minutes. No enemies detected…it's going to be a breeze."

Just hearing No. 1 say that it was going to be a breeze made it seem like it really was. It was their first descent attack, but it would probably go well. They had No. 1. As long as they followed what they did during the training…

"Don't let your guard down. You're approaching enemy aerial territory."

"You're always so worried, Ms. Command."

Only No. 1 would be able to talk so casually with Command. Consistently the best in both academics and battle, she refused to let anyone come close to her power and mobility. She was the ultimate YoRHa model. That was No. 1.

"The new canceler is working as w—"

What had happened? The sounds of an explosion had replaced No. 1's voice. It was happening nearby. The transmission had suddenly cut off. That's the only thing that was certain…

"No. 1 is under fire!"

Even though she could hear Yotsuba's frantic voice and No. 16 incredulously exclaiming "What?!" No. 2 wasn't able to accept what was happening.

The flight unit that had been in front of her had vanished. Shifting her gaze, she saw a ball of fire dropping toward Earth. No. 1. "No…" a whisper escaped her.

This couldn't be happening. No. 1 had been shot down.

"What's happening?!"

No. 21's voice was muffled by more explosions. Looking over her shoulder, No. 2 saw another flight unit was missing.

"No. 12 is under fire!"

"I can't!" screamed No. 4.

"To think they would attack during our descent…"

In contrast to the frenzied voices before, No. 21 spoke quietly. How was No. 21 able to stay so collected, even though she was probably devastated as well? And as explosions were going off around them all the while.

"No. 13, No. 14 under fire!"

It was Yotsuba again. And this time they shot down two at once.

"No. 2, calm down!"

She knew. But she couldn't. There was no way she could stay calm when so many of her comrades had been killed so suddenly. It was impossible.

"No. 22, under fire!"

Again. Again, another one was shot down. She couldn't think straight. So much so that reports from Command that "Permission granted to engage in battle on orbit path," and "Attack source detected," sounded like gibberish to her.

Just then, in all the ruckus, she thought she heard a phrase she understood. Was it her code number?

Did somebody call me? Why? Why me?

"No. 2? Answer me No. 2!"

"Y-yes!"

"Following mission procedures, the role of captain will be transferred to you."

"M-me?"

"No. 2, please approve the authority transfer."

She recalled that there was a decision for her to become captain in the unlikely event No. 1 was lost in battle. Their numbers were consecutive, so it was only natural. Still, that was only supposed to happen "in the unlikely event." The probability of that happening must've been something like 0.001 percent...

"No. 2!"

"Yes! Roger that!"

She had to stop overthinking things. First, she had to escape the current situation. To pull through with everybody left. That was the only thing she needed to focus on.

The current situation? Under fire from surface-to-air lasers. What about the cancelers? Not working. And the shields? Not working either. So? They had to rely on the naked eye to evade.

"Everyone, don't lump together!"

If they were all in a tight formation, they made an easy target. They had to diffuse enemy attacks at least until they landed.

"Spread out individually!"

The flight units instantly dispersed. The units that didn't make it fell to Earth, shrouded in flames.

"Command! Where's support?!"

Futaba had said that they had determined the source of the enemy lasers. Command had even relayed an order to blow up the entire island. The only thing left should have been to carry out the order.

"We will reach a fireable position in five seconds."

No. 2 was frustrated to hear Yotsuba's voice. Her comrades were getting hit right under her nose.

"Please hurry!"

The ground was still far away. After what seemed like an eternal five seconds, No. 2 heard Command's order to fire. Another two seconds. A white column of light rose from the point of interest, then the delayed sound of an explosion.

"Enemy fort, sunk."

But that was not the end. After a brief moment of relief, Yotsuba shouted, "Incoming heat source detected!"

"Twenty-three short-range missiles!"

No. 2 heard the commander order them shot down.

"R-roger that!"

They were near ground. If they could evade this, they could land safely.

"Initiating equipment F15! Everyone, let's go!"

The flight unit switched to maneuvering mode—from a form meant for mobility to a form meant to overwhelm as many enemies as possible.

"Initiate counterattack!"

They readied their weapons at once. Each flight unit had a specialized weapon suited to their user. No. 2 and No. 4 wielded laser blades; No. 16 was outfitted with a rail gun. Now the issue was how many missiles they could shoot down before they hit.

"Distance 21000."

First, No. 16's rail gun engaged the missiles as No. 21 calculated and uploaded the predicted projectile paths.

They had started with a dozen other comrades. Now there were only four units against twenty-three missiles. No. 2 suppressed her feelings of anguish and swung at the missile path. The shock wave released from the blade made contact with the missile. There was no time to confirm its destruction before targeting the next one. She swiftly adjusted her aim and fired off another attack.

"Seven shot down. Sixteen missiles remaining."

She could hear Futaba's voice. It sounded indifferent, just like the training.

"Distance 9000."

There was still time. The laser blades howled and the rail gun roared.

"Three missiles remaining."

Just a bit more. How much time was left? Was there enough? Just then, No. 2 heard No. 21 yell, "They're coming!" No. 2 also raised her voice.

"Evade!"

"We won't make it!" snapped No. 16. At this point, there was nothing else they could do but brace for impact.

"Activate magnetic field–resistant skins!"

Though evading the missiles was now down to luck, the androids had a way to protect themselves against an EMP burst. But this would be the first time the magnetic field–resistant skins were deployed during a sortie. They were untested in battle.

It's all right, they worked well in training, No. 2 reassured herself. She thought about the smiling people that had risked their lives during the field experiments.

"The missiles have hi—"

Yotsuba's voice was cut off. There was a blinding flash of light. A powerful magnetic wave swallowed the surroundings immediately after.

[1208/08:05]

"Wake up, No. 2."

No. 2 sat up as No. 16 poked at her. *How weird for me to be sleeping on my stomach*, she thought. And it was rare for No. 16 to come wake her up.

"Good morning… Ah!"

The moment she realized she wasn't in her own room, she recalled that she was on a mission.

Apparently she had lost consciousness from the missile impact. She was probably slammed down into the ground, hence her awkward position on her stomach. That said, all her senses were intact and she wasn't experiencing any mobility issues. Thinking back to the probable size of the EMP, the magnetic field–resistant skins must have been even more effective than as in the field tests. Passing out was a result of her own neglect…

"Don't be such an airhead."

No. 2 was about to apologize, but quickly stopped herself. What they needed right now were not words of apology. She quickly scanned the surroundings. No. 4 was next to No. 16, and No. 21 was behind them. No other comrades in sight. Of course, that included their captain No. 1.

"Si-situational analysis, please."

"Yes," said No. 21 as she positioned herself before No. 2.

"Attackers No. 2 and No. 4, intact. Gunner No. 16 intact. Scanner No. 21, myself, intact. The four models above have successfully infiltrated enemy territory. With the loss of No. 1, the captain, all responsibilities of the captain have been delegated to No. 2. "

There was no new information in No. 21's report, even though she had specialized skills in data collection and research. Put simply, they were in the worst possible scenario she could've imagined, and pretty much helpless.

"That's all, captain."

They clearly wanted a response, but all No. 2 could do was grimly nod at the news. No. 16 blew up in rage.

"Stop dillydallying No. 2! You're the captain, you know?"

"I know but…" No. 2 was clearly at a loss. She must have been wearing an extremely worried expression, because No. 4 gently placed a hand on No. 2's shoulder.

"It's not like we're in immediate danger."

Her hand was warm. No. 2 realized that she felt at home whenever No. 4 was there not only because they were alike, but because No. 4 was caring. In contrast to No. 4, No. 16 had no mercy.

"What are you talking about, didn't you see No. 1 die?"

No. 2 felt her chest tighten. No. 1, who had always been there, was gone.

"Get your act together!"

She knew what No. 16 was trying to say. After all, what they needed now was a strong leader.

"What should I do…I can't be a captain."

She couldn't. *Why me*, she thought. Why did she survive, and not No. 1?

"No. 2. If that's the case executing the mission is impossible. We should tell Command to abort."

"Oh! Yes! I think that's a good idea!"

It was just like No. 21 had said. Why hadn't she thought of that? Her thoughtlessness was shameful.

Of the sixteen androids deployed, twelve had been destroyed. The projected acceptable number of losses for this mission was four. Nothing was going to plan. Even in terms of troops remaining, continuing was impossible—regardless of whether she was capable or not.

"Then I'll initiate a transmission to Command. There is jamming, but the laser transmission is back up and running."

No. 21 opened the transmission interface.

"Report to Command. Please copy."

Though heavily muffled, they could hear Futaba's voice reply, "This is Command, over."

"Command, under these conditions continuation of the mission is impossible. Out of the sixteen of us, only four are still functional. I'll repeat. We request the abortion of this mission."

"This is Command to the YoRHa squadron. We prohibit the abortion of the mission."

"What?"

She thought she misheard the transmission because of the static.

"We order the continuation of the mission with minimum personnel."

She hadn't misheard. They looked at each other.

"But that's…"

She couldn't think of what to say. They had lost more than two-thirds of their squadron. Did Command understand what situation they were in? There was probably some kind of miscommunication.

"This is an order."

With that, their processing circuits instinctively stopped. This was the end. Even if it was some kind of miscommunication or misunderstanding, there was no going against Command's orders.

"This will conclude all communication through laser transmissions."

Following Yotsuba's words all the static disappeared, and silence ensued.

After a pause, No. 21 said, "We've been cut off."

"I can't believe it!"

No. 4 tilted her head back in exasperation.

"We have four units. They're telling us to continue with four units?"

"I don't think it's feasible."

No. 21 replied indifferently. On the other hand, No. 16 made her anger apparent.

"Shit! We lost twelve!"

No. 16 snatched her goggles off in fury. No. 4 pointed at them.

"Hey, taking them off is against military regulations, you know?"

"Look who's talking!"

At first glance, it looked like the YoRHa squadron had black blindfolds wrapped around their heads. But these were not just black pieces of cloth, but actual goggles with heads-up displays about the targets the user was looking at.

So while it was a crucial piece of equipment on the battlefield, at times it was constricting and stifling. No. 4 was intentionally wearing her goggles crooked so she could keep one eye uncovered. No. 16 lashing back at her was well warranted. No. 4 would probably say that the goggles had slipped off or something of the sort, but in reality No. 2 thought she did it because they were annoying to wear.

Anyway, the relatively tame argument between No. 4 and No. 16 about their goggles didn't last long.

"Wait," interrupted No. 21.

"Machine heat signals detected. The number is—no?!"

"No. 21? What happened?"

After No. 2 urged her on, No. 21 inhaled sharply and continued.

"The number of heat signatures detected is approximately 128,000 units."

Everyone froze. They had never even fought that many during training. Because...

"That's more than eight times the size of the predicted enemy force."

No. 2's goggles started to pick up the heat signatures too, which were calibrated for close combat. It really was an unbelievably huge force.

"We got to do what we got to do!"

No. 16 readied her assault rifle. "Right…" No. 4 mumbled. No. 2 pulled out her military sword, thinking that No. 1 would have said a few words right then to spur the squadron.

"No. 4, let's go!"

"Leave it to me for support!" yelled No. 16 from behind. No. 2 felt like she needed to get in front of No. 4. No. 1 had always fought like that, protecting her comrades. No. 2 wanted to at least emulate her fallen leader. If she couldn't become as strong as No. 1, then at least she could become a shield for her comrades.

The first wave of enemies came forward. Their bodies were grotesque, with two long, thin legs protruding from their torsos.

And while they were bipedal, their gaits were slightly off. From legs that bent at close to 90-degree angles to bodies that contained the head within the torso, they were more insectoid than humanoid.

"So these are…Machines."

No. 2 forcefully cut them down, driven by an innate hatred, rather than just the fact that they were enemies. She wanted to cleanse them from her sight.

The Machines toppled over so easily it was almost disappointing. Their behavior and their gaits were hideous. Just when No. 2 was about to fling her sword down to put an end to those she had thrashed, they quickly spun around and stood up. It seemed they had just lost their balance because of their high centers of mass, and had hardly taken damage.

No. 2 swung her sword wildly. Machines collapsed and got back up again. She wanted to cry, because she knew her actions were futile. Still she whirled the sword in all directions. There was nothing else she could do.

When she looked over her shoulder, she saw No. 4 struggling. No. 16 was having a hard time too. They were hitting their opponents, but inflicting little damage.

Why me, she thought again. *No. 1 should have survived, not me. No. 1 would have come up with some gambit to turn the tide in our favor...*

If not, maybe No. 3. She had recorded the most kills during the training, and would have faced all these enemies without hesitation. Or No. 5, who was the fastest YoRHa. Or No. 11, who could use both gun and sword. Or No. 14, who used multiple guns simultaneously.

Why? Why was she here? She wasn't strong or exceptional, just mediocre.

Before she knew it her attacks were deflected. No. 2 awkwardly fell on her bottom. the Machines crept closer with jerky movements.

"Sorry. I can't..."

"At this rate we'll all be dead," muttered No. 16. The Machines drew nearer.

"We won't let that happen!"

The Machines in front of her suddenly collapsed. She thought she could hear gunfire. Somebody had mowed down the Machines. They lay on the ground, motionless.

"You all get out of the way!"

As if that were a cue, unfamiliar androids streamed in. Probably older models, and ancient at that. They wore clothes that completely disregarded temperature. The guns they had equipped were also clearly of antique vintage. But yet, the androids were killing off Machines as if it were a game.

"Use your thermo sensor! The cognitive unit swims in coolant. That's their weak point!"

The only thing she knew was that these women had come to save them from their predicament...

"R-roger that!"

She wasn't going to be dead baggage for her saviors. No. 2 stood up, and readied her sword.

"Thermo sensor, on!"

Just as the unfamiliar androids had said, the Machine heat signatures contained a peculiar cooler spot in their torsos.

"There's the weak point."

She stepped forward and closed the distance with the nearest enemy. She thrust her sword at the section with the lowest temperature. It didn't feel any different from before. But after its long legs trembled for a moment, the Machine stopped moving.

"I…beat it?"

She heard a series of explosions beside her. It was No. 16. Once they knew their weakness, it was easy. All they had to do was fight just like they had done in the training.

The waves of enemies that had once seemed endless gradually dwindled. No. 2 started to think that victory was possible.

"New enemy signals detected. It's their reinforcements!"

No. 21 had sensed them first via radar. The signals showed up on No. 2's goggles after a slight delay. The number of reinforcements was far greater than the number of enemies they had destroyed.

"There's no end! At this rate, we'll be wiped out!"

No. 4 screamed the near identical words that were going through No. 2's mind. Even her tone of voice, on the verge of breaking into tears, was similar…

"Withdraw!"

It was the same android that had alerted them to the enemy's weakness. On her cue, all the other androids began a systematic retreat.

"It's going to plan."

"As expected, Rose!"

It seemed that the leader android was named Rose. Rose glanced back at her comrades.

"Gapera, what's your status?"

"Preparations complete. I can blow them away at any time."

"What's happening?" No. 16 questioned Rose.

"We drew all the enemies to one spot. You were all a big help."

They gathered all the enemies in one spot…to wipe them out? Did they set some kind of trap?

"If you don't want to be blown into smithereens with the rest of them, retreat! Hurry!"

A smaller android pulled her arm as she scolded No. 2. She didn't know her name.

"R-roger that. Everyone!"

No. 21, who seemed to understand the situation, nodded and started running. A hesitant No. 4 and discontent No. 16 followed.

"Land mine!" Rose yelled.

"Okay! Let's do it! Everyone, lie flat and brace yourselves!"

No. 2 followed Gerbera's order and lay flat on the ground. Immediately after, a roar, vibration, and shock wave assaulted them at once.

"So this is a land mine," mumbled No. 2. It was her first time seeing such an old-fashioned explosive in action. She had knowledge about it, but had never used it during training.

The thick smoke covered her line of sight. But through her goggles, she could see moving heat signals beyond the smoke. The enemies were beginning to retreat.

Eventually No. 21 reported, "No Machine heat signatures in range." *We survived*, No. 2 thought. She held back No. 16, who was obviously still wary about the situation, with a glare. Then No. 2 thanked Rose. Without them they would have surely died.

"Thank you for saving us. We are…" No. 2 started to introduce their group.

"I don't recall saving you."

"What?"

Rose raised her right hand. The guns of her comrades, which had been shooting Machines just a few moments ago, were now pointed at No. 2 and her squadron.

[1208/08:37]

They're clearly a suspicious bunch, thought Anemone. They were wearing frilly clothes, entirely unsuited for battle. To top it off, the clothes were all black. That would have made sense at night, but provided no advantage now, during the middle of the day. Their black blindfolds also seemed fishy.

When her leader Rose had told them they would use "that bunch" as bait to blow away the Machines, Anemone had hesitated because there was the small possibility that they were allies. But Rose had made the right call. Using this group as a lure hadn't bothered her at all.

"Who are you?" Rose asked calmly, but the dingy bunch replied aggressively.

"You wanna go, punk?"

The one carrying a rifle was obviously ready to fight, and the one with the crooked blindfold looked back at them with suspicion in her eyes.

"Please stop!"

The one that screamed the loudest was the naive one who had thanked them.

"We are your allies! We're the newer models! The squadron name is YoRHa, I'm Attacker No. 2, and this is No. 4. That's the Gunner No. 16, and Scanner No. 21. I don't know—"

Anemone cut off the member that was allegedly called No. 2.

"We didn't receive any report that such a squadron was coming."

"Our mission was top secret, so I assume no one on Earth would know about us."

"Hmmm top secret, eh?"

That was a smooth reply. If they declared it was "top secret," they wouldn't have to explain it. It was something Command would do. That was one reason why the resistance didn't trust Command.

"If it's top secret, then there wouldn't be any problem in killing you now either."

Anemone quickly slipped behind No. 21 and put a knife to her. *I would only need two seconds to kill this sluggish tramp*, she thought.

"Anemone!"

Anemone loosened her grip, following none other than Rose's command. But not enough for her to return to her place.

"Stop it."

"But…"

Even though Rose was her leader, she couldn't accept the order. "Yeah," said Lily, who agreed with Anemone.

"There's a possibility that they're humanoid Machines."

Recently, the Machines had been evolving at an alarming rate. The lot had been evolving to meet the challenges of the war for two centuries, but the velocity at which they improved themselves had been surging as of late. As Lily had said, it wasn't unthinkable for Machines to appear and take the form of androids.

"You! Don't be a fool!"

No. 16 rushed at Lily. Before Anemone could attack, Shion stepped in front of Lily to protect her. If Shion were to be described by ancient terms, she had a "motherly" aspect to her.

"Stop it! Don't touch her with your dirty hands!"

"What'd you say! You!"

"This will be interesting," Dahlia quipped as she pulled out her sword. No. 16 pulled out her knife. Anemone could tell that though No. 16 was technically a gunner, she had considerable skill at close combat as well.

"Just stop!" Yet again, No. 2. In between a shriek and a cry, her voice carried rather far. She must've been desperate. Whether she was actually desperate or not, Anemone had no intention of listening to her. She was going to continue the fight.

"Dahlia, Anemone, don't," Rose interrupted.

"But, Rose…"

Before Anemone could object, Rose turned toward No. 2 and them.

"We don't want to question you either. But…"

With her gaze still locked on the dingy group of four, Rose took a step back. Seeing that, Anemone could tell that Rose had not let her guard down either. She had probably held back Dahlia and her so that they could initiate a battle with better coordination if it was necessary. Anemone gripped her knife and waited for her next order.

"Recently there have been sightings of suspicious enemy activities. We can't trust you, complete strangers, even if we wanted to. Even if what you said was true, and you are newer models, we don't have the means of confirming that information."

"What? Are you trying to negotiate?" No. 4 said in a joking tone, and flipped her palms up.

"Don't move!"

"You too, stop acting so strange!"

"Whaat?!"

Dahlia and No. 16 started to argue.

"Please wait!"

No. 2 stepped between them. "Shut up!" yelled No. 16.

"Move! I'll shoot you too!"

No. 16 was not bluffing. Even Anemone, who was technically an enemy, could tell. But it seemed that No. 2 could not. No. 2 suddenly started to reach for No. 16's rifle.

Is this girl stupid? Anemone thought. She probably intended to stop No. 16 by force, but suddenly grabbing a rifle was a reckless move. If she did that…

A bullet fired. Anemone could see No. 16, her eyes wide, over No. 2's shoulder. The bullet had grazed No. 2's ear. A few of No. 2's hairs were charred and shorter than before. If the shot had been a few millimeters off and to the side, No. 2's ear would've been torn off. And if the shot had been a few millimeters off and down…

It grew quiet. Everyone had imagined what could have happened.

"We…" No. 2's voice was trembling. "We were a group of sixteen. We were intercepted during our descent…our cancelers weren't working. Everyone…was shot down…one after another…"

No. 2 stiffened up. At the moment, there were No. 2, No. 4, No. 16, and No. 21. The other twelve had died. It was a simple but devastating act of subtraction.

"We requested that our mission be scrubbed, but it wasn't approved. We have no reinforcements either. Command told us to continue in our current state."

"Us" probably referred to the four of them. This was not the first story they had heard of Command being unreasonable. But if this story was true, they were heartless. If it was true, that is.

"What we need right now are comrades! Please understand!"

"They're desperate," mumbled Erica. Sonia furrowed her brows.

"Are you saying that we're similar, because we were both abandoned by the moon?"

The human board on the moon had for a long time been unavailable for communication. Anemone and her group had tried to contact them many times, but to no avail.

"So we're in the same situation. All right. Everyone, lower your weapons."

If it was the leader's order, it was absolute. Anemone put away her knife. Dahlia clicked her tongue, and reluctantly sheathed her sword as well.

"We will hear you out. My name is Rose."

Because of the old weapons they used, when Rose said, "We are a group of older android models." None of the four looked surprised.

"We are survivors from the Eighth Descent Attack."

This time, all four of them gasped. No wonder. It was a mission from two hundred years prior. Most likely before any of them had been created.

It was the largest descent attack ever assembled, with 160 androids deployed to Earth—ten times the number of No. 2's original troop. Regardless, the enemy had outnumbered them, and the mission ended in failure. Since none of them returned, it was recorded that the whole squadron had been killed…in the database.

Some of it was true: they had descended, been surrounded by an overwhelming number of enemies, and their numbers had been slowly ground down by the enemies. But it was not total elimination. There were survivors. Anemone was one of them.

The survivors established the resistance, with Rose as the captain. They used completely different methods than those they had learned during training, and battled their way toward the creation of an Earth-bound base. After that they prioritized the restoration of the transmission facility, and eventually made communication with the moon-side human board possible. Now they would be able to call for reinforcements, and even if it took time for them to arrive, the resistance could scavenge some materials to survive for a bit. Everyone felt relieved.

But there was no reply from Command. They adjusted their location and tested different frequencies during their multiple attempts to make contact. But Command persistently ignored every single attempt from Earth.

It eventually dawned on them that Command had no intention of saving the survivors left on Earth. They had been abandoned.

That said, they had to keep fighting. This was enemy territory. The moment they put down their weapons, they would be killed. They needed to fight to survive.

The battles dragged on, and the resistance was slowly driven into a corner. They lost numbers, one after another. In battle, in an accident, from chassis or cognitive malfunction—as well as via a weaponized logic virus unleashed by the enemy.

Rose, of course, would be moved by hearing that the group of four had been senselessly ordered to continue their mission. After all, Rose, as captain, was the one that had been tortured by overwhelming hopelessness and a doomed future.

That was why Anemone decided to stay wary of the group. It was always better to have at least one person on guard…

[1208/09:07]

The resistance took No. 2's group to a camp on Mount Ka'ala. The trees grew dense, and from above there were no signs that anyone resided among them. The battle two hundred years before had collapsed parts of the mountain terrain, which provided an abundance of locations to hide the small resistance group and their weaponry.

The overgrown foliage obstructed sunlight, creating a dim area even in the daytime. The air was damp, saturated with the smell of mud and moss.

"It's been a long time. We've been fighting here for a looong time," said Sonia, as they walked along. Her way of speech reminded No. 2 of a child. As a member of the resistance, Sonia was a soldier who had survived many harsh battles, but she didn't show it.

Or perhaps that signified how strong she was, considered No. 2. Two hundred years in this place—much longer than she or any of her comrades could imagine—and Sonia had still been able to keep her childishness.

No. 2 herself had been panicking because Command hadn't replied to their transmission. She was still worried, even now. The transmission conditions were poor, and all they could do was keep sending unheard missives.

Ten kilometers away from our destination, we encountered and merged forces with the local resistance.

That was all they had to say. Had Command received it? No. 2 missed the voices of Futaba and Yotsuba. She had never engaged with them in casual conversation, but they had been there ever since her training had begun…

While No. 2 was thinking such thoughts, No. 21 was busy explaining their situation to the resistance in a collected manner.

The objective of this descent attack was to destroy the servers maintained by the machines. Deep in the bowels of Mount Ka'ala was a server that controlled all the Machines in the Asia-Pacific region. There was one entrance to the server room. They had to board the elevator at the top of the mountain and make their way down.

The descent attack being organized with only sixteen androids was a result of this fact.

Using infrared sensors from orbit, Command determined the elevator was an older model with a limited carrying capacity. The number of people that could infiltrate the server rooms at once was limited.

But if they succeeded in destroying the server, the effect on the war would be tremendous. While their enemies were in chaos, the androids could seize control of the whole Pacific Rim. Maximum reward for minimum expenditure. That was the mission.

"…those are the circumstances."

Sonia, who had been sitting on the side, yawned quietly as if bored by the talk. No. 21 glanced over at Lily, but quickly looked back and continued her report.

"Did everyone understand what I said?"

"An elevator, huh?"

Dahlia's tone was, as always, edgy. She was making it known that she was only listening to the story because the leader had ordered her to, and not on her own volition.

"The top of the mountain? I don't remember ever seeing anything like that."

"The entrance is disguised as a boulder. We had a tough time detecting it with infrared sensors from orbit. We went through tens of thousands of images to—"

"We don't need to hear about that."

Sonia bluntly interrupted her. Sonia, like Lily, had probably had enough. That said, not hearing the whole explanation was irresponsible. While they couldn't reveal military secrets, it was imperative to cover everything else as thoroughly as possible—that was surely what No. 21 was thinking too.

"But if the elevator descends from the top of the mountain, then that must mean it passes near the spring water. But we've been there to collect water, and we've never heard an elevator. We've never detected a heat signature in the area either."

It was Shion who made the long counterargument. She was the soldier who had stepped in between No. 16 and Lily, and yelled, "Don't touch her with your dirty hands!" Even now, Lily was leaning on Shion as they both sat.

No. 2 thought the two had a strange relationship. It was understandable for the captain, Rose, to display a parental relationship to Lily. But Lily and Shion were just squadron members, and thus ultimately peers. Why was there a need for one to protect the other? Did the resistance instruct their members to operate in such a rare manner?

"The elevator does not run straight down. More accurately, the elevator runs in a screw motion, which is an ancient mechanism that reduces momentum…"

"Again! We don't need to hear about that stuff!"

No. 2 was fairly certain that the woman who had burst out in irritation was named Erica. She kept saying, "Get to the point!" during No. 21's explanation. She spoke as if the long-winded explanation was somehow all a ploy to distract and deceive the resistance. No, it wasn't just Erica. No. 2 could tell that the other members were getting angry, just from the looks on their faces.

It was then that Margaret spoke up. During the land mine explosion, she was the one who had said, "If you don't want to be blown into smithereens with the rest of them, retreat!" and pulled on No. 2's arm to guide her to safety.

"In other words, unless we destroy the server, our enemies in the Pacific will remain active and organized, right?"

No. 2 emphatically affirmed Margaret's question.

"Yes! That's right!"

That was the central point of the story. Control of the Pacific hinged greatly on whether or not they could destroy the Mount Ka'ala server. *As long as they understood that part*, No. 2 thought. Just then, Rose, who had been quiet this whole time, spoke up.

"How did you locate the server?"

"That's…"

No. 2 hesitated.

"That's a military secret. I can't tell you."

And to be completely honest, No. 2 and her comrades had not been told that information either. Other than the fact that locating the server took an exorbitant amount of resources and time.

They had heard that the reconnaissance squadron, which had been deployed before them, had located the server. They hadn't been notified of the reconnaissance squadron's well-being since. So No. 2 had thought to herself that they had all died.

Total elimination was a phrase that would make anybody uncomfortable. Command most likely decided to keep the news a secret since it would affect morale. Of course, this was only No. 2's hypothesis.

"What do you mean?" Anemone asked cynically. But No. 2 couldn't just directly say, *The previous squadron was probably totally eliminated, so we didn't receive the details.*

"That's the important part too."

Erica mumbled, from beside Anemone. Even Margaret, their sole supporter, was furrowing her brows.

What should I do… No. 2 panicked. She searched for words that would persuade them. But before she could find them, No. 16 burst out in fury.

"Whatever! This is a waste of time!"

"Wait! No. 16!"

No. 2 followed No. 16, who had started to storm off with big strides.

"Wait!"

No. 2 was ignored without a second thought. No. 16 strode farther and farther away at a disheartening pace.

"Wait, please!"

She ran and ran, finally catching up. She grabbed No. 16's arm, but was quickly batted away. This time No. 2 ran in front of No. 16 to make her stop.

"I think if we explain just a little more, they'll understand!"

No. 16 didn't answer. It was No. 4 who answered in her stead. "For how impatient No. 16 is, she waited pretty long, don't you think?"

What she said seemed to have irritated No. 16 even further. No. 16 glared back at No. 4.

No. 21 sighed.

"It's no use."

"No. 21? What do you mean?"

"If we can't elicit their cooperation, we'll have to carry out the mission ourselves."

"What? But you just said that we'd definitely fail with only us…"

No. 21 was the one who had suggested they request a mission abort.

"We will probably fail. The difference in force between us and the Machines is clear. As such, I requested a mission abort."

"Yes. So that's why…"

"Anything other than a mission abort is the same to me. Everything else is a lost cause. Whatever we do is futile. Whether we work with them or not, the result will be the same."

"That's not true! If we join forces, we can succeed!"

"And your reasoning is?"

She didn't want to jump to conclusions. If a possibility existed, even a small one, she wanted to bet on that.

"You see? There's a sea of possibility awaiting you."

Strangely enough, No. 2 recalled those words. That person couldn't have known this situation would arise, but ever since that conversation the word "possibility" had taken on a deeper significance to No. 2.

Either way, "betting on a possibility" was probably not enough "reasoning" for No. 21. At the very least, she wouldn't acknowledge it.

"You don't have a reason, do you?"

No. 2 had nothing to say. "That settles it," No. 16 said in a spitting tone of voice.

"But! Something like that!"

She had to stop them. Four people would amount to nothing. She didn't want to die in vain. She wanted to avoid that at all costs.

"Wow, wow. Is this a falling-out?"

Dahlia was poking fun at them. Looking over her shoulder, No. 2 could tell the other members of the resistance shared Dahlia's sentiment.

"Stop it, Dahlia. Rose wants to talk," chided Gerbera. Next to her were Rose, and the other resistance members.

"W-what do you want?"

No. 2 braced herself, because she thought they would point their guns at her again. After all, Rose had kindly told them that they'd listen, only for No. 2's squadron to ruin the conversation.

But Gerbera had said that Rose wanted to talk, instead of jumping straight into an attack. *What talk?* thought No. 2.

No. 2, who was at this point hurriedly trying to deduce the nature of this talk, was totally caught off guard by Rose's words.

"We'll accept your request. We'll cooperate."

"What?" yelped No. 4. No. 2 froze, her mouth open in shock.

"I told you we'll help. Did you hear me?"

"Y-yes. I heard you."

"I think it's hopeless either way," muttered No. 21 from the side.

"No. 21, don't say that. Let's bet on the possibility for now. Okay?"

No. 4 had articulated No. 2's feelings.

Indeed, they had no reasoning that would satisfy No. 21. But Rose and her members had accepted them. They had trusted No. 2… or so she wanted to think.

"Hmph," No. 16 snorted.

"We'll fight with you."

"What kind of tone is that!"

"What?"

Margaret separated No. 16 and Dahlia, who were starting to argue yet again. Margaret looked gentle, but observing how Dahlia would unconditionally listen to her made No. 2 think otherwise.

"Are you all okay with that?"

Rose moved to the front of her group. "From now going forward, I prohibit all hostility toward these four individuals."

It looked like Dahlia and Anemone scowled. But even though they looked like they wanted to say something, there were no rebuttals.

Erica, Shion, Gerbera, and Margaret wore somewhat tense expressions, and Lily and Sonia were openly displeased. Yet all the women nodded. They would follow their leader, putting any suspicion and discomfort aside.

That was how much trust they put in Rose. No. 1 had been a slightly different type of leader, but Rose was probably a good leader as well.

"We are comrades fighting for the same cause!"

"Comrades," mumbled No. 2. What they wanted the most, in unfamiliar enemy territory—they had obtained just that. It was difficult to say that the others trusted them as of now, but their leader had promised they'd fight together. So it would probably go well.

They were going to succeed, no matter what…

[1208/09:31]

"What are you two doing?"

Rose's exasperated question brought Dahlia and No. 16 back to their feet. They had been on their stomachs, hands clasped, seeing who was stronger. It was called "arm wrestling" back in the human civilization days, and was a particularly popular activity because it didn't need any extra equipment or much space. But neither No. 16 nor No. 21 knew about this activity—most likely because they were newer models, and information exchange between their comrades had been sparse.

Anemone and her group had known about "arm wrestling" because one of their comrades had been programmed with simulated memories. The more time they spent together, the more stories they heard. Even if those stories were simulated.

"Dahlia, if you've got time to play around…"

Dahlia replied, breathless. "I. Just finished. Showing. How strong. I am. To this fool."

No. 16 retorted, also breathing heavily. "What…are you saying? It's. Your. Utter. Loss!"

"What?"

"Hmm? Come. at me!"

"That's enough!" Rose scolded.

"If you have time to play around, go gather some water!"

That's right, Anemone agreed silently. They were being so irritating. Since the number of meatheads had doubled, the number of distractions had also doubled.

"Then I'll be the one to go gather it. Since I'm faster!"

"What?! I'm definitely faster!"

"It's a race!"

"Don't be a sore loser!"

Dahlia and No. 16 dashed off.

"You two! Don't forget the water tank!"

"Gosh! They're so irresponsible."

Margaret chased after them with the tank. It was finally quiet. Anemone sighed. They were getting along pretty well.

It had been nearly an hour since Rose announced their allegiance. They had just finished giving the newer models a tour of the camp. It was too early to let their guard down.

"We're going to exchange information. No. 2, No. 4, Sonia, come with me."

After Rose took the three of them away, Anemone, Shion, Lily, and No. 21 were left alone. While Anemone was grateful that the noisy ones were away, now it was too quiet and a bit awkward.

Anemone wasn't good at small talk to begin with. She couldn't find any meaning in exchanging irrelevant words. That's why she felt relieved when Lily started talking to No. 21.

"You don't have to wear your blindfold?"

"I take it off during non-battle situations, since it's irrational. And it's a set of goggles, not a blindfold."

"Is that right?"

"Isn't it hard to move when your vision is obstructed?"

No. 21 turned nonchalantly toward Lily. Lily took a step back.

"What's the matter?" No. 21 asked with a puzzled expression. Anemone couldn't blame her. She didn't know how wary Lily was.

"Well…the YoRHa are a bit scary."

At this point, Anemone thought that wariness was necessary. Being a little scared was perfect. Not like the meatheads that started to get along in no time at all.

"You're scared"

"It was just us for a long time, you know? We're like family. For other androids to show up is…"

Lily hid behind Shion.

"Sorry, Lily gets scared pretty easily," Shine replied, in lieu of Lily, who had her lips shut tightly. "She always has nightmares at night too."

Shion chuckled, as she glanced back at Lily. "I can't help it," Lily said, pouting.

"I see a lot of nightmares at night. Sometimes I feel like I'll die in the nightmare."

"You can't be killed in a dream," pointed out No. 21.

"You're quite irrational."

"You don't know that! Ghosts might appear too!"

"Ghosts don't exist either. You're just trying to run away from your real fears. Most likely your fear of Machines."

Listening halfheartedly to the trio's conversation, Anemone determined No. 21 to be a brainy type. Now that she thought about it, No. 2 had called No. 21 "Scanner No. 21." Maybe her explanations were so long-winded because she specialized in intelligence gathering and research.

"I'm scared of both. Ghosts scare me, and so do Machines. I'm so scared that sometimes…I think I'm human."

"Human?"

This was the first time Anemone had heard this. She knew Lily was cowardly, but she hadn't known that Lily suspected herself to be human.

"I see dreams, and have emotions. Why am I not human?"

"Because you're not a living being. Our bodies are artificial."

"But if we break, we die, you know? I'm scared of dying. I'm scared…"

Lily trembled. Even though Shion attempted to comfort her by telling her it was okay, Lily kept repeating that she was scared.

Anemone, as well as all her comrades, feared their destruction. It was an emotion hard-coded into their programming to promote higher chances of survival.

But for Lily, that fear was stronger than that of the other androids. Whether or not creating a model capable of experiencing extreme fear was the result of intention or error was unknown.

"No. 21," said Shion, suddenly. "You all are new models, right?"

"Yes. This is the first time our models are being deployed on the field."

"If you're newer models, I wonder if you have greater tolerance for fear."

"I'm not sure. It's not like we can measure that."

Just like humans, androids were capable of hiding or faking their feelings, so measurement was out of the question. Anemone was about to sarcastically say that measuring wasn't the same thing as understanding, when…

"Show yourself!"

She had felt a presence, and drew her gun.

"Don't shoot me!"

No. 4 appeared, with her hands above her head. Anemone clicked her tongue and put her gun down.

"Eavesdropping? Serves you right."

"No. I left everything to No. 2 and came back."

"Then don't do anything misleading like sneaking in."

No. 2 and No. 4 were both apparently attackers, but their personalities were completely different. Anemone didn't like either of them. She *couldn't* like them.

"Jeez, Anemone. There's no enemies, so no need to be so uptight."

"Shion. We had tons of comrades who died just like that. Don't you remember?"

They had been too careless. Not just Shion, but Rose, Dahlia, and the other members of their troop.

"Are you also afraid of dying?" No. 21 asked, her head tilted to one side. As if she couldn't imagine Anemone being scared of death. That irritated Anemone, and she flung the question back at her.

"Aren't you scared?"

That was probably petty of her.

"I am scared. Death means you're nothing. Your body, consciousness, they both disappear from the world. That is something that's very frightening."

"I am too."

That said, Anemone had an inkling that No. 21's fear and her own fear were slightly different. No. 21's fear seemed more irrational, and her own was more instinctive and emotional.

Well, either way, the important thing *was* to fear destruction. That inspired caution. It discouraged actions with avoidable risk. For example, trusting an unknown group that identified themselves as newer model androids.

It was best to keep their distance from the four of them. Anemone was going to walk away, but No. 21 turned around first.

"Where are you going?" Lily asked her as she was leaving.

"I'm going to check up on the surroundings. Just scanning is not the same as actually seeing for myself."

Lily, who had been hiding behind Shion this whole time, trotted off to catch up with No. 21. Anemone's eyes were wide with surprise. What Lily said next really shocked her.

"Can I come with you?"

"If you're not scared of me."

"Okay. I think I'm getting used to you."

Anemone looked over at Shion, who was still and had her mouth agape. Recently, Shion spent more time with Lily than Anemone. Her surprise must've been greater than Anemone's.

"Wait! I'm coming too!"

Shion scrambled after the two.

"Then me too!"

No. 4 stopped, and looked back at Anemone.

"You aren't coming?"

Without answering, Anemone stood up and turned her back toward No. 4.

"Okay, then I'm gonna go."

From her tone of voice, it didn't seem like No. 4 took it sourly. Anemone heard a "See you later" from behind her. She kicked at some dirt. It felt like she was being really childish by herself.

[1208/10:02]

No. 4 left after Rose had finished explaining the vicinity's topography, the attributes of common enemies, and the weapons and equipment the resistance had on hand. She said she would "take a look around," so it wasn't as though she had left without warning.

Besides, she hadn't left because she got bored of the discourse. She had most likely gone to check what the other resistance members were doing.

It was hard to tell from her casual way of speech, but No. 2 knew that No. 4 was not as frivolous as she seemed. Talking a lot was her way of gathering information. As such, No. 4 was surprisingly well aware of her comrades' personalities and actions.

But whenever No. 2 point it out, No. 4 would avoid the topic. She always blew it off by saying she just liked cute and exciting things.

Either way, her nature was often misunderstood. Especially by people who she'd just met.

"I'm sorry about my comrade's selfish actions."

Rose replied generously to No. 2, who had her head down in shame. "I don't mind. I explained the important parts. The rest, including exchanging information, is just details."

Rose's smile as she said, "I don't mind," reminded No. 2 a little bit of No. 1. No. 1 was also generous.

"You said that…you've been fighting here for a long time, right?"

Sonia nodded. She was the one that had said, "It's been a long time."

"Without any help?"

It was Rose, not Sonia, who answered that question.

"The only people you can trust on the battlefield are your comrades. Not that we have many left at this point."

No. 2 had heard that 160 androids had been deployed on the Eighth Descent Attack. The number of androids left in the resistance was in the single digits. They had lost the rest.

"What about Command?"

She had hesitated to ask. She was scared of what the answer might be. But she asked anyway.

"We've been abandoned by the moon."

As expected, the answer No. 2 didn't want to hear. Sonia shrugged and continued.

"All Command kept saying was "top secret," "top secret," "top secret." Only that. We knew they wouldn't be much help, but still, to be actually abandoned…"

"But, still you fight."

"Because that's what we're made to do."

Cleanse the Earth of the Machines. That was their purpose, No. 2 knew that. The question was whether or not she could actually execute.

"We have to take back the Earth, for humans…"

"No. Not for anyone else. For ourselves. Our comrades are pretty much family. We fight to protect our family. It's only natural, right?"

Family. It was a foreign concept to No. 2. She found it extremely odd that Lily and Sonia called Rose "big sis." Even though she knew what "family" and "big sister" meant as words, she didn't understand them.

They're different from me, No. 2 sighed internally. Not just because she couldn't fathom the concept of a family; aside from that, Rose and the late No. 1 both had determination and a sense of responsibility that she didn't have.

"As expected of a captain. I…I can't do it."

"Of course you can. You showed some guts back there. You risked your own safety to shield your comrade, and contain her temper."

Realizing that Rose was talking about her breaking up the fight between Dahlia and No. 16, No. 2 shook her head. She hadn't intended to "risk her own safety." It was all in the heat of the moment.

"You sounded sincere."

"What?"

"You were sincerely trying to survive with your comrades. That made me want to cooperate."

She had been desperate when she had screamed, "What we need right now are comrades!" She had just spat out some random words that came to mind. Those words had swayed Rose…

"Those weren't my words. I was just repeating something I'd been told. Someone taught me that joining forces with allies is the key to victory. Those words have been stuck in my head ever since."

She could hear the voice in her head. That person had taught her many things. Thinking of them, a warmth spread though her chest. But it didn't last. As soon as she realized that person was gone, the warmth disappeared.

She would never see them again…

"You're almost like a human."

No. 2 looked up in surprise. She had been told a similar thing before, by the very same person she had been imagining.

"Have you…seen humans?"

"No, I've never seen them directly. I've just heard about them. Don't you hear about them a lot?"

When Rose and her companions had been manufactured, there had been rumors and stories about humans. No. 2 felt a bit of a generation gap. A difference of two hundred years was no small amount of time. No. 2 rarely heard stories of humans.

"I just thought you were similar to the impression of humans I got from back then. Well, I might be biased, because I want it to be true."

"Want?"

"I want to meet humans. I want to live as the humans do… It's a very common wish."

Androids, regardless of when they were made, had an innate affection and admiration for humans as an emotional support to carry them through the harsh war with Machines.

Perhaps the resistance, which had been fighting on Earth, had a greater attachment to humans compared to the new YoRHa. Fighting for two hundred years meant two centuries of worshipping humans.

"Is that why you call each other by names?"

"That's right. I named everyone. So that we could communicate with each other as humans."

"I see."

This was another one of the things that No. 2 had thought was odd. Aside from a select few that made significant contributions on the battlefield, most androids were only assigned a code number, and they called each other by those numbers. Single digits were attackers, the tens were gunners, and the twenties were scanners. The system was created so that specialization of an android could be determined instantly by their number.

No. 2 had assumed that all the resistance members were given their names due to their meritorious accomplishments, but it turned out Rose had just named them herself.

"I'm thinking of naming you all as well."

"Fantastic!" Sonia squealed at Rose's suggestion. No. 2 frantically shook her head.

"N-no. Please don't!"

"Why?"

Sonia cocked her head.

"That's...uh, wasteful."

"What? No it's not wasteful."

She had no right to have a name, not without having produced any results. Besides, Command was in charge of honorific naming. It wasn't something androids should do of their own volition. Even if they had the right to perform honorific naming, they had to fill out a request form, and get approval from the board. But she hesitated to explain that to Rose. What could she say?

"After the mission, please."

What came out was just an excuse to delay the incident. But it was better than confronting her outright, No. 2 thought. At the very least, it wouldn't make things awkward.

If, after the battle, both No. 2 and Rose's group were alive, and No. 2 had to tell them the real reason, she would let them scold her all they want—that was, if they were alive.

"I see…"

No. 2 was startled by Rose's tone of voice. Did Rose see through her? That by saying after the battle, she had stuck in a tiny fragment of hope.

"I'll think of a good name for then."

No. 2 was relieved that Rose had ended the conversation at that.

"Hey, can I help you brainstorm? No. 2's impression, let's see…"

It seemed that Sonia wanted to continue the naming conversation. No. 2 sighed internally.

"Rose! Kalmia and Clematis are here!"

Gerbera brought two unfamiliar androids with her.

"That's rare for Kalmia to show herself. What happened?"

"When I told her about the newer models, she said she wanted to see for herself."

Gerbera glanced back at the two behind her. One of them made a big nod. Which one was Kalmia, and which one was Clematis?

"Are you the new model?"

Caught by surprise, No. 2 nodded after a slight delay.

"I'm Kalmia, a weapons merchant. This is my secretary Clematis."

Weapons merchant? Was it accurate to literally interpret the title as a person that sold and bought weapons? Currency economics had existed a long time ago. She remembered hearing that the occupation of merchant disappeared along with the collapse of the system…

"And you are?"

"I am code number No. 2."

"What's your name?"

She bore a small grudge, as Kalmia brought up names yet again. "I don't have one," she answered. Sonia interjected from the side.

"She's going to get one after the mission. I'm going to help brainstorm too."

Even though she hoped the introduction of new faces would veer their conversation away from names, they were back at it again.

But it didn't go how No. 2 expected. Their conversation was cut short as they heard a cry in the distance.

"Screaming?"

Rose didn't stay around to listen to someone say, "It's Rose." Sonia and Gerbera followed. Unaware of what had happened, No. 2 blindly chased after them.

[1208/10:23]

Ashamed to face anyone, Anemone had walked away from everyone else.

But it was times like this that she would inadvertently run into people. This time as well—she ran into No. 21, Shion, Lily, and No. 4. They said they would "take a look around," so it wasn't too great a coincidence when they encountered Anemone loitering around the camp grounds.

That was fine. It was her fault. But then No. 16, Dahlia, Erica, and Margaret appeared. They had just come back from gathering water. What bad luck. She'd run into eight people at once.

Still wanting to be alone, Anemone was slowly backing up when it happened.

"Ugh. Ah…ahhh!"

Lily collapsed, clawing at her neck. Erica screamed, "Don't touch her!"

Anemone held back No. 21, who had tried to run toward her. She released the safety on her gun.

"She's infected."

Right as everyone save No. 4 and No. 21 aimed their guns, Rose appeared. She understood what had happened at a glance. Rose gave Anemone a signal with her eyes. Sonia and Gerbera drew their guns.

"What are you doing! Stop it!"

No. 2 jumped in front of Lily. *This idiot again*, Anemone thought to herself.

"No. 2! Don't go near her! It's an infection! She must've contracted the logic virus from the last battle!"

The logic virus that the Machines spread could all of a sudden over-write data in an android's cyberbrain. Then it would destroy the android's consciousness and take over their body.

"What about the shield? Is it not working?"

No. 16 tilted her head to the side. The newer models might have them, but Anemone and her generation did not.

"Lily!"

No. 2 carelessly approached, but Lily pushed her away. Her body-control system was already affected. There was no way to prevent further infection, or save her. There was only one thing to do: kill her before the infection progressed and she went rampant.

"Wait!"

But this time it wasn't the idiot, No. 2.

"Aren't you all family? Lily said so. Are you going to watch your family die?!"

No. 21 stood in front of Lily. Dahlia shouted.

"Move over! We're going to shoot you too!"

"I won't! I can't accept her death without trying anything!"

"We're doing this because there's nothing we can do!"

"I can! I'll eliminate the virus!"

"There's no way…"

Dahlia's words were cut short. Looking up, Anemone could see No. 16's gun aimed at the back of Dahlia's head.

"No. 16, stop."

Rose spoke up.

"Once you're infected, there is no cure."

"Shuddup! If No. 21 says she can do it, it's possible!"

Using her voice as a cue, No. 2 and No. 4 held Lily down. They moved without hesitation. They mumbled, "Reprogramming, start," as No. 21 started typing on her terminal. Lily's body jerked off the ground. No. 4 screamed.

"What is this strength?"

Lily's right leg tried to kick No. 4, who was holding down the left leg. Anemone's body had started moving before she could think.

"Anemone?!"

Rose's voice brought Anemone back to reality, realizing that she had thrown her gun away and was holding down Lily's right leg. No. 4 was right—Lily was impossibly strong.

"The ghosts are coming… Nooo!"

Lily's voice was strangely cracking. The infection was spreading to her vocal mechanisms. Were they going to make it?

"There's no such thing as ghosts! I'll fix you!"

Lily's legs kicked up in the air, as if they were disagreeing with No. 21. Before she knew it Anemone was sent flying back. With too little time to brace herself, Anemone groaned as she hit the ground with full impact. Yet she still got up. She had to contain Lily, or else No. 21's procedure would be interrupted.

As Anemone stood back up, swaying, she saw Dahlia and Margaret already holding Lily down. "Captain!" Dahlia cried.

"I don't want to lose anyone else!"

Dahlia, Anemone, and the rest of the named androids had killed comrades that were infected by the logic virus before they became a threat. They couldn't do anything else.

But if there was a way to save them without killing, they wanted to bet on that possibility. Killing comrades didn't get any easier after the first time; in fact, it became harder with every comrade they had to end with a bullet to the head. If there was another way…

"But…"

Rose probably felt the same. But being the leader, making the decision was a lot harder.

"Rose! Trust us! Isn't protecting your comrades the responsibility of the leader?" No. 2 said as she held down Lily's shoulders.

But suddenly No. 2's expression grew strained. Anemone wanted to ask what had happened, but before that she felt her own face pucker up into a scowl. It was hard to breathe, let alone talk. Her lungs were about to burst.

"Gravity…attack…" Dahlia said, her voice a low moan. She had been knocked off her feet, and was pinned to the ground. Anemone was also on her stomach, unable to move.

"This is bad! She's starting to acquire enemy attacks!"

As expected of a newer model, No. 4's voice was the same as usual. They probably had better resistance to gravity attacks than the older models.

"No. 21! How much longer?"

No. 16's voice carried panic. "Just a little more," said No. 21, as she removed a small chip. Lily tried to bat it away.

"No!"

No. 2 clung on to Lily's left leg. She couldn't move because of the gravity attack. Anemone desperately dragged herself toward Lily. She grabbed Lily's right ankle. No. 2 held on to the left leg. If they could hold down Lily's legs, they could restrict her movements…

"Installing data!"

No. 21, who had finally moved behind Lily, raised the chip in the air. It most likely contained a vaccine program.

"Please! Come back, Lily!"

Lily's beast-like howling drowned out No. 21. No. 21 wrapped herself around Lily to stop her writhing. Their bodies intertwined and fell down.

Right as Anemone started to suspect that the vaccine had failed, her body lightened. The gravity attack stopped.

No. 2 and Rose rushed forward at once. Rose lifted Lily into her arms, as did No. 2 for No. 21.

"Virus eliminated from the central nervous system. Force rebooted."

While she was slightly out of breath, No. 21 was as calm as always, to the point where Anemone thought she could be a little happier.

"Big sis?"

Lily looked up in confusion at Rose. It seemed she didn't remember how she got there or what she had been doing.

"You were infected by a virus. No. 21 returned you to normal."

Lily's eyes opened wide, and looked over to No. 21.

"I told you. That I'd…fix you."

No. 21 was calm, but clearly exhausted. She leaned her head on No. 2's shoulder and closed her eyes.

"I told you it'd be okay." No. 16 said a little boastfully, which Dahlia followed up by poking No. 16's head.

"You were panicking too, weren't you?"

"Shut up! You wanna go?"

"What did you say? Bring it on!"

Margaret sighed, "Again?" as Dahlia and No. 16 started to squabble again. This time, Anemone didn't feel as annoyed.

While she wasn't planning on getting close with them, Anemone decided she would acknowledge the new group. They had kept her from having to kill a comrade. That was an act of pure sincerity…

[1208/14:14]

It was a quiet early afternoon. All of a sudden No. 21 was standing beside Anemone.

"You don't have to rest?"

"Yes, I'm okay."

The newer models probably recovered faster too.

"What about the others?"

"They're in a meeting with rose. About tomorrow morning's mission."

"Ah, I see."

The mission for infiltrating the server room via the elevator at the top of the mountain was set for tomorrow morning. Given their capabilities, the YoRHa would be vital to mission success.

"What's wrong? Did something happen?"

From No. 21's profile, Anemone thought she could see that something other than fatigue was bothering her.

"Aren't you tired?"

"No, that's not it…"

No. 21 faltered. Anemone urged her on with a look. She was being uncharacteristically nosy.

"I was thinking, in terms of close combat, there's not much a scanner can do. Is there even value in someone that can't contribute?"

Ah, so that's what it was. If a battle broke out tomorrow, it would most likely be close combat. The road to the mountaintop was narrow, and the elevator was also cramped. No. 21 was worried that she would be useless in that situation.

"And you're asking me, of all people?"

Anemone returned even more cynicism to No. 21, who had been unknowingly cynical.

"For two hundred years, I haven't been able to finish off the Machines."

It sounded self-deprecating. Both Anemone and No. 21—no, perhaps Anemone even more so than No. 21—were useless puppets.

"I've unable to die for two hundred years. And yet I wanted to live. Even though I wasn't valuable in the least."

"I'm sorry. I didn't mean it that way."

"I know."

No. 21 had no ill will. Words with no ill will became cynicism when they were true.

"From the time we entered the stratosphere and landed on the ground, I've lost many comrades. But I'm alive, somehow. Does luck determine the value of a person?"

"Do you feel guilty? If you feel bad about living, there's a simple solution. Kill yourself, right this instant."

Anemone held out her gun for No. 21. This was ill-willed cynicism.

"I can't do that. I have to make sure the mission succeeds, for my fallen comrades as well."

"Then don't ask."

Whether or not their individual existences had value, or whatever reason they had to live, there was no choice. It was a foolish question, to ask something she already knew the answer to.

"You'll know when the time comes. Even if you don't want to know."

"You're probably right. No, you *are* right."

No. 21 shook her head and corrected herself. Anemone kept quiet. She didn't know what else to talk about.

It's not that she was being wary. All her suspicions evaporated when they saved Lily. In fact, Anemone was glad she didn't have to take the initiative and talk. Put simply, she was bad at conversation. Whether that be small talk or in-depth discussions of research.

Thus, No. 21 was the one to break the silence.

"There's really nothing to see on Mount Ka'ala, is there?"

"It's been that way. There's nothing there."

She lied, just a little. Back when there used to be night and day everywhere on Earth, this very spot looked out at a crimson sky and sea, or so she had heard. But that was before the Earth's axis had tilted, so it was a description from ancient times. Even before Anemone and her squadron had landed on Earth.

"Have you always been like that?"

No. 4 appeared from behind No. 21. When did she get here? She had approached them without making a sound.

"What do you mean?"

"You seem so bored. Just like the view from here, nothing there. Have you always been like that?"

"Who knows?"

No. 4 asked some stupid questions.

"I don't remember what I was like before."

"Androids should have customized simulated memories though?"

Perhaps she was influenced by No. 4, but No. 21 was seemingly interested in this irrelevant topic. "I forgot," said Anemone, deciding it was better to let it go.

"Huh? Doesn't that mean there's something wrong with your brain?"

Anemone felt her shoulders drop. She just didn't like No. 4.

"Why are you all so prying?"

"Because we're interested."

"Leave me alone," Anemone replied, as she turned away. Yet No. 4 continued the conversation without regard.

"If we lost our memories, would we be different people? If we lost our memories and we became different people, would that still count as living on?"

"I didn't lose my memories."

"Oh, so you *do* remember."

"This is stupid."

"Are they stupid? Fake memories?"

What value did fake memories have? They never happened in real life, so they weren't practical, like real experiences.

"Memories are just baggage in our artificial brains."

"But memories meant a lot to humans. They treasured them. They weren't baggage in human brains. Maybe, unbeknownst to us, there's a significance to them."

No. 21 even says sentimental things sometimes, thought Anemone, taken by surprise.

"But once you die they disappear. That's the kind of thing memories are."

Anemone hissed those words, wanting to put an end to the useless talk. No. 4 and No. 21 didn't say anything else.

[1208/15:44]

"Is there anything else we need?"

"Mines. They're completely out."

"Ah, that explosion. What a reckless bunch. Don't you think so, Clematis?"

Upon hearing those words, No. 2 deduced that Kalmia and Clematis were doing an inventory check of the weaponry and gunpowder. Apparently she had accidentally come across the pit the resistance used as an armory.

No. 2 softened her footsteps as she stepped back. It would be embarrassing if they found out she had gotten lost in the camp when it wasn't even that big to begin with. But Clematis's words stopped her in her tracks.

"Something is wrong with Rose."

"What do you mean?"

"Please look at this."

"Hm? Isn't that number wrong? There's an extra digit."

What was off by a digit? Even though she knew it was bad to eavesdrop, No. 2 strained her ears.

"No. There's no mistake that this is the amount of weapons she ordered. That's why I thought it was strange."

No. 2 knew that Rose had ordered weapons from Kalmia. No. 2 was there when she'd done it. But she didn't know the specific number. Rose had just said, "I'll send you the list, could you gather them for me?"

"It isn't new for Rose to be reckless, but this number is just absurd. It's almost like…"

Clematis hesitated to go on.

"It's almost like?"

"It's almost like she's planning for an all-out war. Their final battle."

"Don't be so dramatic."

"I understand, but…"

"An all-out war? Against the Machines?"

"Looking at the order, that's the only thing I can think of."

"Are you crazy? Or maybe you're being deceived by the messengers from the moon."

From the moon? Are they talking about us? No. 2 instinctively clutched her chest. Her breathing was tense. She couldn't. They would hear her. At this rate…

No. 2 backed away, careful to not make a sound. After she was far enough, she ran. She was still struggling. There was a dull pain in her stomach.

Rose is going into her last battle? Because of us? No, Rose isn't such a rash person. Clematis is probably misjudging. Or maybe she's being overanxious.

But, actually—am I sure about that? Aren't I trying to reject Clematis's words because I don't want to bear the responsibility of them? No, that can't be. Rose would never choose to put her comrades in danger. The weapon order is large because us four came. That's got to be it…

She had no clue where she had run off to. Suddenly, she almost butted heads with No. 21. No. 2 could barely keep a scream in.

"No. 2?"

No. 21 said with a puzzled look. Next to her was Lily.

"Uh…so, you were here."

"Did something happen?"

No. 21 was sharp. No. 21 ignored that, and turned to Lily.

"Lily, are you feeling better now? Is it okay for you to be walking?"

No. 2 had tried to smile, but perhaps her goggles hid her eyes, and it didn't come across how she wanted. Lily hid behind No. 21.

I didn't mean to scare you, was what she wanted to say, but Lily's glare made her shrink away.

"You may be No. 21's captain, but Rose is my only captain!"

Lily announced that and turned around.

"No. 2, I'll report you later!"

No. 21 followed Lily. Unable to fathom the situation, No. 2 was left standing on the spot. What Lily had said, that "Rose is my only captain," was stuck in her head.

"I know that."

She didn't need to be reminded that she wasn't captain material. She just didn't expect to hear it from a member of the resistance. That meant it was obvious to people outside of her squadron as well…

"Just as I thought, captain is too much responsibility for me."

She suddenly felt tired, so sat down right where she was standing.

"You're being all weak again."

She heard a familiar voice. She wanted to cry.

"I can't do it. Seed, I can't."

She had never wanted to be with Seed as badly as now. She wanted to see her one more time. She wanted to cry and tell her about her fears—and she wanted to be scolded by her.

By the person that had taught her many things.

[11941 11 15~]

"Duck!"

She was pushed to the ground as soon as she heard the warning. Her head was pinned, her nose in the dirt. The moment she tried to raise her head, she heard an explosion. A heat wave rushed over her back. She got goose bumps after realizing that she would've been hit directly had she not been ducking.

"What are you doing, wandering around like that. Are you an idiot?"

The android that had pushed No. 2 down was clearly an older model.

"Th-thank you. Sorry about that."

"What are you doing here?"

"Uh, well…where am I? I got lost."

She was going to be reprimanded, she knew it. How the hell could an android get lost? She thought she would be suspected as a defective model. But her reply was unexpected.

"Well, I'm not surprised."

"What?"

"This is an experimental area that simulates conditions where location data is not obtainable."

I see, thought No. 2, relieved. She had lost track of how far she had walked and which direction she was heading in, so much so that she was about to cry. But apparently that wasn't due to her incompetence.

"But how did you get in here? It doesn't look like you're an experimental subject or a staff member?"

"W-well, I got lost."

"Huh? In this small orbiting base?"

This time for sure she expected a scolding, but again she was wrong. She burst out laughing. No. 2 stared at her, surprised.

"You, would an android say that?"

"I'm sorry…"

"I thought you were joking at first, No. 2."

She laughed again.

"You know about me?"

"Yeah. I know about you YoRHa very well."

No. 2 widened her eyes in shock. Why? Who was this android?

"I'm Seed. An older-generation experimental model."

Seed was apparently in charge of the weapons and equipment for the YoRHa squadron. It made sense—no wonder she had data of No. 2 and the rest of the YoRHa as well.

"From up close you really do look like humans, don't you?"

"Have you seen humans?!"

"Yep."

Seed had said that so nonchalantly, but to No. 2 it was so incredible she seemed almost divine. There were very few androids that were allowed to meet with the humans on the moon. The more androids that came, the more bodyguards needed. Therefore, for an android to have seen a human meant that it was one of the chosen few. Just thinking of it made No. 2's heart beat faster.

And that wasn't all. Seed had more to say.

"I lived with humans, shared experiences, and stormed the battle-field with them."

"Battlefield?! You've been to Earth?!"

"Only three times."

"Wow!"

Only three times? That was a lot. Seed was a veteran who had fought on Earth three times. And unbelievably, No. 2 was talking with her right now. Her excitement made her babble a bit excessively.

"We're also going to Earth soon but I'm a bit worried…"

"Hey, hey, isn't that a top secret mission?"

"Oh! That's right!" She covered her mouth with her hand in a hurry.

"You're funny. If you're bored come again. I wanted someone to talk to. Oh, don't enter the experimental area though, okay? You wouldn't last," Seed said with a snicker.

The Earth is blue.

The first human to see the Earth from space had said that, Seed taught her. Apparently she was just passing down information. She had heard the story from some of the humans on whose side she'd fought.

"But from the ground, it's not blue at all. Everywhere you look is the color of sand. I felt duped."

For her first landing, Seed had touched down in the desert. She had apparently landed in the middle of a sandstorm and fought Machines there.

"After the battle with the Machines, I was told to look up. I was so beaten down, I just wanted to go home, so I was like why am I doing this—and when I looked up the sky was blue."

The sandstorm had passed. The blue sky extended forever, nothing in its way, recalled Seed, nostalgically.

"Earth from space and space from Earth are both blue. Even though neither of them are actually blue. Isn't that interesting?"

"Are you still worried?" Seed asked, staring at No. 2's face.

"I'm worried, but now I'm looking forward to it too."

No. 2 occasionally sought out Seed between her trainings. She was told to come see her again, but No. 2 genuinely wanted to see her. Even though she was a "chosen one" who had fought alongside humans, she was really openhearted and friendly. It made her happy.

At times she would whine or confide in her about her worries, but Seed never criticized her. She always teased her by saying "You're whining again?" but her tone of voice was gentle and her eyes smiled when she said it.

On this day, Seed was again telling her stories of her battles on Earth as she was repairing her chassis. Apparently there was a specialist that performed maintenance on her chassis, but she chose to do it herself unless there was a serious issue.

Seeing her expertly swap out parts for her right femur was exhilarating.

"Ms. Seed, why did you…"

"You don't need to use a Ms., just Seed is fine."

It made it feel like they were a bit closer, which made her happy. She decided to ask her a slightly rude question. They were at the point where she didn't have to worry about formalities, and could focus solely on her curiosities.

"Seed, why did you take over the role of testing new equipment?"

"Is it weird?"

"No, that's not what I meant. I've heard that the experiments can be…pretty rough."

There were often many blemishes in the prototype equipment, and the experiments, which simulated various situations, put quite a bit off stress on the chassis. Not to mention older models had less durability relative to the new YoRHa. To be honest, it was extremely dangerous. Then why did she want to take part in such a thing?

"Well, I should be retired by now, after all."

Seed's chassis was covered in scars. Perhaps they had stopped production of her original parts; much of her body used parts that were obviously not of her original design.

"I left everything on the battlefield. Do you understand?" she asked, to which No. 2 shook her head. She had never even been in a battle, so she couldn't imagine a battlefield either.

"Anger, sadness, fear, and even happiness. I have none of it now. There's nothing in this empty head of mine." Seed looked down at her hands. "But when I'm holding a weapon, I forget all of that. Even if this is a simulated battlefield."

Considering Seed's point of view, why did No. 2 feel a bit of sadness? It was hard to imagine Seed, a celebrated warrior, being sad.

"What are you doing?" barked the commander.

No. 2 rushed to salute her. The commander looked over at Seed and No. 2, and slightly cocked her head.

"Seed, it's rare for you to be talking to a new model."

"She's interesting to me."

"No. 2? She's a mediocre specimen lacking extraordinary qualities."

"Sorry," No. 2 said, as her shoulders drooped. Just as the commander had said, she was average in every way and had nothing she was exceptionally good at. No. 2 knew it too well.

"An average model, huh. That's good."

"What?"

What did she mean? What could be good about being an unexceptional model?

"Being average means she has the potential to improve in every way."

"Potential…"

"I guess you could say there's more room for hard work to factor in. You can improve any aspect of yourself with hard work and adaptations. You can decide how you want to improve."

She had never thought of it like that. A boring, unexceptional model. That's what she thought she was.

"You see? There's a sea of possibility awaiting you."

All of a sudden, it was almost as if she could see a bright light in front of her. But it was too bright. At least, too bright for now.

"And a person who knows they're average is strong."

"Strong? Me?"

You know that you can't accomplish things alone, so you try to engage the help of others. You know how to trust and treasure your comrades. That's the strength of an average person."

It didn't click for her, even if she was called strong. Seed saw that, and nodded, "Yeah, well, it's okay if you don't understand now. Just remember that you can win if you fight together. That's enough for now."

Then Seed looked over at the commander standing to the side and gave her a knowing look.

No. 2 couldn't believe it when she heard that Seed had died, even though the news came straight from the commander.

She replayed the message from the commander over and over. She thought she was being pranked. She thought a laughing Seed would appear on the screen saying, "Were you surprised? Sorry." That's what she believed. It's not like she had evidence, she just believed that was the case.

"Hey No. 2. You still alive?"

Seed was laughing, like always. See, she was still alive. Her dying was just a joke after all…

"If you're seeing this message, then that means I'm no longer a part of this world."

She stopped breathing. She thought her heart would stop beating too.

"Unlike humans, we're told that androids have no souls. This message is the closest thing to a soul that I can leave you with."

"No…" Her voice sounded far away.

"Due to the invasion of the Machines, and the human retreat to the moon, Earth has virtually returned to a state of nature. Looking at Earth now, filled with greenery, I'm starting to think that humanity were the bad guys…"

Seed stopped talking. She looked down, as if she was thinking about something, or was trying to remember something. She spoke up again.

"Recently I've been thinking. If my memories of living among humans are real. If they're artificial, what are we fighting? I don't know anymore."

She remembered Seed's face when she had said, "I have none of it now." She had a sad expression, unbefitting of a strong warrior.

"No. 2. I don't want you to become like me. I want you to find a reason to live."

A reason to live? She didn't know what Seed meant. She didn't know what she was saying, or what she was being told to do, because it seemed like she'd never see Seed again.

"Thanks for talking to me. Goodbye."

After Seed disappeared from the screen, No. 2 couldn't move. It felt like something within her would collapse the moment she moved.

"This message was recorded before she died. In case something happened to her."

Seed was dead. No. 2 said that over and over in her head, but it wasn't sinking in.

"What happened?"

"An accident during an experiment. The new equipment failed."

The new equipment she was referring to was probably the magnetic field–resistant skin. Seed had said that her experiment would protect the latest generation from all EMP attacks.

"I can't believe she died!"

No. 2 had planned to visit Seed right after returning from the descent attack. She wanted to talk to Seed about Earth. Tell her how she felt when she looked up at the sky. How she felt when she stepped on the green Earth...

"I know! Aren't there spare chassis?! What about her personal data backup?!"

Even if her original body was gone, as long as they had her personal data they could upload it to a temporary body. That way, No. 2 could see Seed again. But the commander's words destroyed any meager hope that No. 2 had.

"This is already a decided matter."

"But!"

"We can't fix her."

"Wait! Commander!"

"That is all."

There was nothing she could say. No. 2 fell to her knees on the spot.

"No...it can't be..."

Why couldn't they upload the personal data to a spare chassis? Technologically speaking, avoiding death was possible. Yet.

"Why? I can't accept that!"

The commander had already disappeared.

"I can't...accept that..."

Her shoulders involuntarily shook. Pain rose from the bottom of her throat. No. 2 cried alone in a deserted hallway.

[1209/04:59]

Before No. 2 could say, "I can't accept that," No. 16 blew up in anger, yelling, "Are you kidding?"

"We can't approve the deployment of reinforcements. Command wishes for resolution with your current manpower."

No. 2 couldn't hear any emotion in Futaba's voice. Didn't she know she was pretty much telling them to die?

"There are hostiles gathered near the elevator of the server room. Please swiftly make your way to the destination."

They had called for reinforcements precisely because they couldn't do that. The path to the peak of Mount Ka'ala was infested with an unbelievable number of Machines. Even though the troop had embarked before dawn, when they expected the Machines to be sluggish, the Machines were not as inactive as they had hoped.

Furthermore, the number of Machines was not the only thing that was unexpected.

"It's no use! Can't locate the cooled area in their torsos!"

Dahlia's voice contained traces of panic and irritation. Up until this point, all they'd had to do was use their thermo sensors to identify the cooler brain section of the Machines and attack that point. But the enemies today had no distinguishable contrast in heat throughout their bodies.

"As expected. They most likely put some heat-insulating material around their cooled brain unit," No. 21 said, with furrowed brows. The Machines had analyzed their attacks, learned, and come up with a countermeasure...

"We aren't like you, floating safely in orbit! Send us reinforcements already!" No. 16 roared at the transmission device. She was clearly panicked. But the replies that came back through the transmission were blissfully unaware of their predicament.

"I'll repeat. Use the local resistance to protect the YoRHa squadron, and make your way to the elevator."

"What is the resistance to you—just pawns on a chessboard?"

Dahlia's face was red with rage. It was only natural. The lunar stronghold had ignored the resistance for so long, only to use them when it was convenient.

"Let me talk to the commander! I demand an answer from the commander!"

Talking to the operator was getting nowhere. At this rate, they wouldn't be able to reach the elevator, much less destroy the server.

"This is a direct order from the commander."

"There's no way…"

No. 2 was speechless. *This is the second time*, she thought bitterly. Command had given no explanation when they rejected the mission cancellation request. This time too, her call for reinforcements had been rejected without a single concrete reason.

It wasn't like their request was obviously impossible from a technical or time perspective. But Command wasn't lifting a single finger to help. What was Command thinking?

"Leave this to me! Everyone go on ahead!"

Lily's voice brought No. 2 back to reality. Lily had both arms raised, standing in the way of the enemies. The red eyes of the Machines all locked on to Lily.

"Watch out!"

Just as No. 2 saw that Lily was in danger, she felt her limbs weigh her down. That's when she remembered the report she had gotten from No. 21 the night before.

"Sorry! I don't have full control over it just yet!"

Lily yelled with her arms raised. It wasn't just No. 2 and the resistance that were being pinned down. The Machines were also frozen in place.

"Is this?"

No. 2 knew the answer already.

"Gravity wave! Lily can use enemy attacks now!"

Struggling to keep herself from sitting, No. 2 repeated No. 21's words in her head.

The night before—after Lily had told No. 2 that "Rose is my only captain!"—No. 2 had curled up in a fetal position at the edge of camp. No. 2 had felt unreasonably dejected until No. 21 came up to her to explain the situation.

"Sorry about Lily back there," No. 21 said, as she began explaining the series of events that happened within the past hour.

"You ran into her right after she activated gravity wave."

"What do you mean? Why Lily?"

"Logic viruses take over a chassis and make it attack its comrades. The majority of these viruses force the chassis to fight past its natural limit, making it stronger in close combat. But I suspect that Lily's virus was the type to copy its own attacks onto the infected chassis, or perhaps Lily's attack potential was too low and the virus decided to use its own attacks through Lily's chassis."

"W-wait. Sorry. I can't keep up."

"In other words, Lily is capable of Machine-style attacks now."

"That's amazing!"

"That's if she can control them though."

And No. 21 told No. 2 to not tell anyone else, because Lily wanted to keep it a secret for now…

"Wow! They aren't moving!" No. 4 said as she jumped in the air, probably because gravity had returned to normal. No. 2 almost fell on her behind as a result.

"I did it!"

Lily swung her arms in a big circle. No. 2 and the troop were able to move, but the enemies were still fixed in place.

Lily, who had mastered gravity wave, looked back with a satisfied smile.

"Head toward the elevator now! Hurry!"

But Lily's technique was but a way to slow combatants down. It didn't destroy the hostile units. So while the enemies were stuck in place, so was Lily—which meant…

Rose shook her head firmly, as if she had read No. 2's mind.

"We're not going to leave without you!"

They didn't know how long Lily could sustain her gravity wave, but it was most likely not for long. The Machines that were now frozen would start moving after the wave dissipated. When that happened Lily would be left in a horde of enemies, all alone.

"It's okay! I want to be useful!"

Lily stared down the enemy. Her straight posture exuded her strong determination.

"I was a scaredy-cat. I was a useless coward. But you saved me. You told me, of all people, to come back. That's why I want to be useful!"

"Fine," Dahlia replied, as she walked over to Lily.

"I'll support you."

"If Dahlia is staying then I am too," said Margaret.

"Then I'm staying too," No. 16 said, and turned toward No. 2.

"YoRHa squadron gunner No. 16 will now accompany the resistance to defend Mount Ka'ala!"

"But No. 16…"

"No. 2, no, captain. Once we return let's kick Command's ass," No. 16 said in a jesting tone.

"And, if I left it to an incompetent person like Dahlia I would be too worried."

"Who you calling incompetent?" Dahlia replied as she looked back.

"You wanna go?"

"Let's do it!"

Dahlia and No. 16 laughed as they bickered. Now they would have two people for close combat, and two people for long-range combat. Still, it was uncertain whether they would be able to contain the situation…

"I'm against it. Splitting up our forces is dangerous."

Dahlia emphatically interrupted Rose.

"If we all stall here, the mission can't go on! Captain Rose, let us do it!"

That was a good point. Since they couldn't expect any reinforcements, they needed to create an opening. No. 2 agreed that at this rate they would all die. On the other hand, splitting up their already small group was also dangerous. Separate groups might end up being too undersized to handle waves of enemies.

Either choice was dangerous. As a captain, which way was No. 2 supposed to choose…

"Okay. We'll split into two and continue."

If she had been the one to decide, No. 2 would not have reached a decision this quickly. She might've still been hesitating, on the verge of crying. But, realized No. 2, she and Rose had reached the same conclusion. Whatever the chance, if there was even the smallest possibility, they would bet on it.

And she wouldn't want to waste Lily's desire to be useful. She understood how Lily felt, because she also had an inferiority complex of feeling like useless baggage. Wanting to be useful to her comrades. If she had a chance, she wouldn't want to waste it either.

"No. 2, is that okay?"

"Yes!"

No. 2 looked at No. 4 and No. 21. They both nodded. After saluting to No. 16, No. 2 chased after Rose.

[1209/06:01]

The elevator hall was cold. The mountain peak reached a dizzying altitude. Because of that of course it would be cold, but it was freezing past those expectations. It was well suited as the entrance to hell.

Anemone brushed those thoughts out of her mind; it was out of character to be thinking of things like that.

"Rose? What happened?"

Sonia ran around Rose and looked up at her face. Now that she said it, Rose looked more solemn than usual.

"I shouldn't have left Lily and the others after all…"

No. 2 was the one that stopped Rose, who was about to turn around and go back.

"Wait!"

How many times had Anemone seen No. 2 stop someone? She seemed quiet, but in times like this she became heated.

"Lily said she wanted to be useful! She isn't going to be a pawn! Dahlia, Margaret, and No. 16 are all desperately fighting, I'm sure! If we go back now…"

No. 2's voice trembled and broke off. She couldn't say the rest. *How naive*, Anemone thought. But that was okay. She was naive because she had never been betrayed. It was better for her not to experience the pain and despair that came with betrayal. Serious and good-natured, that's how No. 2 should be.

"Okay."

Rose painfully agreed. She leaned against a boulder that was off to the side and peered at the elevator door.

Lily and the rest would die. It was the obvious truth. The death of comrades; they had experienced such over and over.

I want to name us. We're family. Doesn't it feel more natural to call each other by name?

Anemone still remembered the face Rose had made when she first said that. She wore a forced smile. Her voice shook, as if it were being blown around in the wind.

At their feet was a pile of bodies—comrades who had been infected by a virus. That day, they lost five. Their code numbers were strangely consecutive.

Up until that point, losing numbers had tormented them with intolerable sadness. Numbers were cruel. They would be reminded of their fallen comrades by their numbers.

Five code numbers were lost. That hole brought unparalleled pain. A hole, wide and deep.

"How lovely! Like humans!"

"And I'm going to call captain 'big sis.'"

Everybody agreed. They decided to ignore the countdown to a harsh future.

They knew. That someday, everyone would be gone…

"What's wrong No. 21?"

No. 2's puzzled voice brought Anemone back to reality. No. 21 was crouched before the elevator, scowling. Half her face was covered by goggles, so all Anemone could see was her puckered mouth. Her expression made Anemone worried.

"All we had to do was go to the server room…but the elevator won't activate."

"Why?"

"The enemies put up security. I need to release it in order to access the bottom floor."

"No…"

It's okay. I just need to hack it. It's easy."

No. 21 smiled and started to operate the terminal. Anemone thought something was off. Was it really easy? Then why had she seemed so upset a moment before?

"See, easy."

The elevator doors slid open. Rose and the rest of the group entered. Anemone followed. No. 21 didn't budge. Anemone's suspicion was confirmed.

"Go on without me."

"Why? Let's go, No. 21…"

"I want to, but if I stop the operation the elevator will stop as well. I need to stay here and keep hacking until the elevator reaches the bottom floor."

No. 21 said so in a swift manner. Anemone jumped out of the closing elevator.

"I'm staying! On to the server room, everyone! Leave support for No. 21 to me!"

"Okay! I'm counting on you!"

The elevator doors closed on Rose's voice and No. 2's surprised expression.

"Since when?"

Anemone slowly pointed her gun at No. 21.

"You can...tell? I don't dislike how intuitive you are."

"It's not intuition. I know. I've seen many people go through this."

No. 21's body swayed erratically. It was a distinguishing symptom of the logic virus.

[1209/06:20]

Minute vibrations and a sinking sensation accompanied their descent. The only problem was, since the elevator was ancient, the trip was excruciatingly slow.

"I wonder if Anemone is okay."

Gerbera mumbled. "It's okay," No. 2 replied.

"The elevator is still moving, so they should both be okay."

No. 21 had said she needed to keep hacking to keep the elevator moving. The fact that all of them were heading toward the bottom of the shaft was an indicator that the two of them were still alive.

"But No. 21 was infected."

No. 2 and No. 4 gave each other a look after hearing Sonia speak.

"I know. I've seen a lot."

"What do you mean you've seen a lot?"

Gerbera answered instead of Sonia.

"Androids infected by the virus have their motor functions damaged. Their movements become irregular, and..."

No. 2 met eyes with Erica.

"So you mean..."

Erica averted her eyes before No. 2 could finish. Erica had noticed too. Then Anemone must've been aware as well. Anemone had seen just as many infected androids as Sonia and Erica.

"So that's why she said she'd stay," No. 4 mumbled gloomily. Then, they suddenly heard a rumble. It wasn't from nearby. Sonia glanced around nervously.

"What was that?"

The heat source was displayed on No. 2's goggles. She looked at the location—the last known coordinates for Lily, Dahlia, and Margaret—in dismay. And one more person.

"No. 16…"

The temperature and the scale implied that this was no simple explosion. A suspicion that their fusion reactors had acted up crossed No. 2's mind.

"We need to go back!"

She reached for the elevator control panel, but she was grabbed by the back of her neck and pulled away.

"What are you doing? Let me go!"

But Rose grabbed her by the collar, and pushed her against the wall.

"Who chose to leave them there?"

"But—"

"You know what happened!"

Earlier, No. 2 stopped Rose from going back. This time, Rose was trying to stop No. 2 from going back. They both knew…Rose and No. 2.

Of course, No. 2 knew what happened. No. 16 had detonated her fusion reactor in hopes of exterminating the enemies, along with Lily, Dahlia, and Margaret. Infected No. 21, who was still hacking, and Anemone, who had stayed back to kill her. If they pulled back now, all those deeds would be meaningless.

"But I'm…sad. This is…"

"No. 2," said No. 4, as she rested a hand on her shoulder. "Don't you want to fight?"

How easy would it make things if she replied that she didn't— that she had always hated it. Even though she was a soldier, deep down she wished they didn't have to fight. But saying that was prohibited.

"No. 4, aren't you sad?"

"I'm sad. But we need to fight. That's why we exist."

"That's true, but…" Not wanting to bother her comrades. Not wanting to be a burden to her comrades. That was how No. 2 had fought, in training and on the battlefield. Everything she did was for the sake of her comrades, but her comrades kept dying. That was unbearably sad.

"Why do we have the emotion of sadness? Even though we're androids."

"In order to adapt to various situations. Humans, who had no fangs, claws, or wings, were able to emerge victorious via the process of natural selection and thrive due to their adaptability. We were made in the image of those humans—that's what I heard a long time ago. Back when I was still in orbit," explained Gerbera.

"But isn't that a paradox?" No. 4 interrupted. Because she had her goggles on crooked, as always, it was easy to tell what she was feeling from her expression. No. 2 was familiar with the look in No. 4's eye.

"What do you mean by paradox?"

No. 4 turned toward Shion, whose head was turned to the side. Hearing how No. 4 said, "Because," confirmed No. 2's suspicion. No. 4 was trying to change the subject. So No. 2 wouldn't brood over her thoughts.

"Because we were made to do things that humans couldn't do. Destroy the Machines. This is something humans couldn't accomplish."

"Yeah," said Shion.

"That's right. If it's better to be like humans, then we should be like humans. But we're also tasked with doing things that humans couldn't do."

"It's true! It is a paradox!"

The elevator was moving along at a consistent pace. The bottom floor was still a way to go. Gerbera spoke up.

"Perhaps humans wanted that paradox to defy logic. For example, via our simulated memories."

It wasn't only No. 4 that wanted to change the subject. Everybody was trying to find a lighter subject to talk about, especially because they were trapped in such a small space.

"Simulated memories, huh?"

Rose eyes lightened up a little. From that, No. 2 could tell that her simulated memories were filled with happiness.

"Rose was a little boy. A little boy with a military dad."

Sonia said with a chuckle. She had certainly heard of Rose's days as a boy. "Lucky," No. 4 said enviously.

"I was a girl who wore a uniform to school. A high school student. I only have memories about fooling around with friends every day."

"Yours are better. Mine are about being a bullied child." Gerbera sighed.

Compared to Gerbera, her own simulated memories were happier, thought No. 2. Her memories were about living with her grandmother in the countryside—warm and peaceful memories. Her parents passed away early on, so it was just her and her grandmother living together. She "remembered" tending to the fields every day, the feel of the soil, and the smell of grass.

"I only remember growing up on the battlefield. My parents were killed, and I was handed a gun at an early age," Erica revealed with a dark look.

"Me too," replied Shion.

"Apparently Lily had similar ones too. She was always dragging bad memories around with her."

Sonia's words made No. 2 recall when Lily had said, "I was a scaredy-cat." Lily's sense of exaggerated fear must have been born of her memories.

"Sonia was the same. Sonia was always sad and alone. But right now she's Rose's little sister. Sonia and Lily are also both little sisters to Rose. Those are the real memories. That's why I'm not sad anymore."

Everyone was aware that simulated memories were not real. But to the individual, they all seemed real. Simulated memories were just as vivid as, if not more vivid than, the real memories they had.

No. 2's own memories weren't awful, but other people were not as lucky. There were people who struggled constantly from the terrible memories they were given. Just to "be like humans."

"The time we spent together has overwritten our fake memories. By experiencing joy and sadness together, we've accumulated real memories."

Rose patted Sonia, who was standing next to her, on the head. No. 2 understood that this was what a "big sister" was. Her hands had a hidden strength that would protect her family. Those hands existed because she was humanlike.

"Maybe..." started No. 4. "Machines don't have emotions, but if they've acquired them..."

Machines, which simply and emotionlessly executed orders from the server. If they had acquired emotion, if they had begun to experience camaraderie and learned to protect one another, wouldn't they become an even more terrifying foe?

The mere thought made No. 2 shiver with fear.

[1209/06:30]

No. 21's fingers shook as she typed commands into the terminal. The progression was faster than she had expected.

"Aren't you able to eliminate logic viruses? Can't you do what you did to Lily, but this time for yourself..."

"I want to, but it seems the enemy is evolving. They've adapted to my patterns and are resistant to my hacking."

"Right. If you could you would've done it a long time ago. I asked a dumb question. Sorry."

"It's fine," No. 21 replied, her voice strained.

"I'm glad you stayed. Once the elevator gets to the bottom floor..."

"Yeah," replied Anemone. "I'll kill you."

A sigh escaped from No. 21's lips. It sounded like she was relieved or in great pain. Perhaps it was both.

Either way, it wouldn't be long before No. 21 lost consciousness. First her sense of balance would deteriorate. If the tips of her fingers and toes were being affected already, it meant the infection had progressed pretty far.

The limited time remaining slowly whittled away. The elevator's floor display wasn't changing very quickly.

Anemone feared what would happen if she had to kill No. 21 before the elevator reached the server room. That fear irritated her.

"How much longer? Has it not arrived at the bottom floor?"

"Wait. A little longer. Just a little bit."

No. 21's fingers moved frantically. She was panting. She probably would've struggled to just sit up. At the same time, it was depressing that Anemone could decipher how far the virus had progressed. She had seen so many of her comrades die that she could tell the status of the victim from just their mannerisms and expressions.

"They made it."

No. 21 let go of the terminal. Her hands ripped off her goggles. No. 21 slowly opened her eyes.

"Hey, those eyes…"

Anemone was speechless. No. 21's eyes were both blood red. It was a symptom from the terminal stages of infection. It was a miracle she was operating the terminal in this state. It wouldn't have been surprising if she had gone rampant minutes ago. She must have held it together via sheer willpower, to get No. 2 and the group to the server room.

"Please. While I'm still myself."

Anemone leveled the gun at No. 21. She struggled to keep her hands steady.

"Any last words?"

No. 21's mouth distorted into a smile. Or rather, she tried to smile.

"Who would you pass them on to, even if I had any?"

"I'll hear you out. Even if I die right after this."

"I'm glad I met you. These memories are real. Thank you."

"Okay."

"Come on, hurry!"

Anemone quietly pulled the trigger. A familiar pulse passed through her arm. No. 21 flew into the air. Anemone thought she could see a smile on her face. The matter that had previously been No. 21 fell to the floor with a thud.

"I'm coming soon…"

Lily, Dahlia, Margaret, and No. 16 were all dead. No. 21 had told her that an explosion induced by fusion reactors had occurred. The heat signature was just around the size of four exploding reactors. There must have been enemy reinforcements, and they were forced to self-destruct, she said.

It was unknown how many of Rose's group would survive as well. There was a possibility that they were all already dead. In fact, that was more likely. There was no chance that the enemy would leave a server room that controlled the entire Asia-Pacific region unguarded.

Anemone pointed the gun at her own temple. All she had to do was pull the trigger. She could do it with her eyes closed. It was incredibly simple…

She couldn't move. Her hand, which held the gun, was frozen in place. Her finger wouldn't move to the trigger. She struggled to breathe. A cold sweat burst from her pores. Her vision wavered erratically… Her legs were shaking.

"Why?!"

She forcefully moved her arm, which felt as though it had a mind of its own. The gun dropped from her hand. She heard the gun fire. Anemone fell to her knees in defeat. She realized she had thrown away the gun, not dropped it.

Anemone had her hands on the ground and was gasping for air. She couldn't breathe. It wasn't cold, but she couldn't stop herself from shaking.

"What a mess…"

To think she had killed so many comrades, yet was having second thoughts when it came to killing herself. Pull the trigger. That was the only thing she had to do. Just that.

"Shit!"

Anemone searched No. 21's body for whatever weapons she might have been carrying. She remembered No. 21 sheepishly admitting she didn't take part in battles very often. As a result, she wasn't outfitted with anything particularly useful in battle. There was only the most standard equipment: a small-caliber pistol and a knife.

Anemone put No. 21's pistol and knife on her belt. She scooped up her own gun and dashed out of the elevator hall.

If she couldn't kill herself, she would let the Machines kill her. Of course, she wasn't going down easily. She would take as many of them with her as she could.

"Hey you suckers! I'm here! Kill me if you can!" Anemone screamed as she rushed into a swarm of hostiles.

[1209/06:39]

The bottom floor was even more frigid then the elevator hall, and smelled of rust and dust. While it wasn't pitch-dark, the dim light required them to watch their feet when they walked.

"What's that?"

Rose, who was leading the group, stopped. No. 2 strained her eyes to see what Rose was pointing at.

"Humans?"

Rose cautiously moved closer. As they approached the figures, it became clear from their silhouettes that they were indeed at least humanoid. They were small, and were wearing wide-hemmed clothing.

"Red clothes? Girls?"

Two girls wearing identical outfits—a short one-piece in a vivid red that was visible in the darkness.

No. 4 spoke in an unusually deep voice. "Those red girls…they don't look like your average children."

At the very least, they weren't human. Their heat signatures didn't match those of humans, and there weren't any humans left on Earth in the first place.

"*Welcome.*"

"They talk," exclaimed someone. It was surreal for them to look like humans, and also talk. Their voices were raspy and clearly artificial. The red girls were that strange.

"*We are an extremity of Machines.*"

"*We were modeled after your form.*"

It took a long moment to process what the girls had said. Machines. Extremities. It was hard to make the connection between those terms and these two girls.

"W-we need to contact Command…" No. 2's voice got stuck in her throat. No. 4 yelled into her transmission device, in lieu of the struggling No. 2.

"Command! Please answer! Command?!"

The transmission device was dead. No. 4 tried different frequencies and even laser transmission, without a single answer.

"*They won't answer. We're blocking transmissions.*"

"*Because we want to have a long conversation with you.*"

The red girls spun around, as if they were dancing.

"*We were waiting for you to come, this whole time.*"

"*We were watching you, this whole time.*"

The two girls tilted their heads to the side in a mirrored fashion. The girl on the right tilted her head toward the right, and the girl on the left toward the left. The way they acted made No. 2 very uncomfortable.

"*Why do you try so hard?*"

"*Why do you want to die so much?*"

"Don't be stupid!" screamed Rose. "It's because of you fools, isn't it?! You're the ones that stole Earth away from humanity!"

The girls ignored the accusations, and instead started giggling.

"You were only created to die."

"You were only sent to Earth to die."

Wanting to drown out the girls, No. 2 raised her voice in a frenzy. "That's wrong! We came to fight! We weren't created to die!"

The girls scoffed at her reply.

"Even though humans abandoned you?"

"Even though you're being used?"

No. 4 suddenly drew her sword and attacked. "Shut up!"

It was an uncharacteristically intense shriek from No. 4. She was swinging her sword as hard as she could. Perhaps that's why the girls dodged her attacks so easily.

"We hacked into your servers and found some interesting information."

"It's very important, so listen closely."

"The YoRHa squadron were deployed as experimental weapons."

"The unexpectedly severe battles and conditions were anticipated by Command."

"Command wants to use your battle data to create a more advanced autonomous soldier."

"Command planned all of this."

"You're the only ones that survived."

No. 2 was frozen, her sword half-drawn.

"These kids…what are they saying?"

Their request to scrub the mission was rejected. Their request for reinforcements was rejected. Command rejected them, repeatedly, without reason.

"And you still want to fight?"

"And you still want to resist?"

No. 2 was opposed to Command's decision. She had thought it was strange. She kept trying to ignore it, but a doubt had sprouted in the back of her mind since the time Seed had died.

"From the beginning, Command was going to…"

From the beginning they had planned on abandoning the YoRHa squadron. Perhaps Seed was declared dead because she had too many attachments to YoRHa? Or did Seed know all along, and act nice toward No. 2 because she had felt guilty?

"No. 2! Don't be fooled! We don't know if it's the truth or a lie!"

No. 4's voice brought her back to reality.

"We didn't survive for no reason!"

Rose's voice gave No. 2 enough strength to grip her sword again. She was right. How many comrades had they lost on their journey to this subterranean level? Ending this mission would mean that the sacrifices of their comrades had been in vain.

For now, all they had to do was what they were told. They could ponder their existence after they completed the mission.

"*Then fight.*"

"*With this boy.*"

The girls beckoned with their hand. A silhouette appeared from an area that had been empty just a few moments ago. It was a Machine with a body slightly larger than any of the Machines they had fought before, with eight legs protruding out of it. An appearance that could only be described as repulsive.

"Where did it come from…"

There was no time to dwell on the question. The Machine started to move. It manipulated its legs, which were bent at right angles, to move around, giving it a freakish gait. But it was unexpectedly fast. No. 2 could sense danger in the back of her mind.

She promptly turned on her thermo sensor, but couldn't perceive any temperature differentials. Just as they all feared their enemies would, the Machines had studied the resistance's attacks and adapted.

Rose readied her sword.

"Let's destroy it!"

Gerbera, Shion, and Erica all said, "Yes," in unison, as they spread out. After flanking the machine, they began to attack at once. Three of them formed one group, and Rose and Sonia composed the second. On the third flank were No. 2 and No. 4.

They knew it would be a tough battle. Any Machine deployed on Earth was encased in extraordinarily resilient armor. They were far more formidable than any simulated foe androids might face during training. And to think they didn't know what its weaknesses were.

That wasn't all. The eight-legged foe suddenly rose up. Before they knew it, it was on its six hind limbs, and attacking them with the front two.

"Everyone, dodge it!"

The two legs crashed down, their tips leaving deep gouges in the ground. Had she been late to dodge, she would have been crushed, thought No. 2 with a shiver.

She hadn't expected the enemy to use its legs, a means of motion, as a means of attack. And the enemy hadn't slowed a bit since switching to six legs.

Erratic motion, hard armor, and an unexpectedly powerful attack— how were they going to destroy it? And more importantly, how long could they dodge those attacks…

The feeling of desperation, like that had accompanied her first battle on Earth, took ahold of No. 2.

"This one's strong!" Erica cried hopelessly from behind No. 2. Gerbera and Shion were gasping for air. No. 2 panicked, because she knew they would have to end this as fast as possible. The longer they took, the more Rose and her group would struggle. She knew how fragile the chassis of a two-hundred-year-old model could be. Seed had been like that too. Every moment outside of field tests was spent repairing her chassis…

"Erica!" Shion screamed.

"No!"

No. 2 thought she heard the scream of someone nearby, but in reality it was herself. The same unsightly legs had crumpled Erica's left side in one swipe. Red liquid gushed out. It was definitely an instant death.

Suddenly, the Machine crouched. Just as No. 2 processed the motion and braced herself for its next attack, the enemy disappeared from her line of sight.

"It jumped?"

It happened in a flash. The Machine leapt into the air as if it were weightless.

"Gerbera!"

There was no time to stop it. The Machine landed, twisting Gerbera's neck in an impossible direction. At the same time, its front legs assaulted Shion.

Shion, who had been paralyzed in fear, was slammed to the ground. She had been pierced by legs as thick as her femur. She probably had no time to even feel pain.

That wasn't all. The Machine spread its eight legs and splayed itself onto the bodies of Erica and the other troops, looking to crush them all.

"You shit!"

Rose whipped her sword over her head. No. 4 grabbed her arm.

"Wait! It's behaving weirdly!"

Right as the Machine started to move, the bodies of Erica and the others took to their feet. They weren't alive. There was no chance that anyone with a pulverized heart, snapped neck, or gaping hole in their torso could still be alive.

The three of them swayed as they walked. No. 2 had seen those movements before. Slight irregular swaying, as if they were being pushed around by wind.

"Were you…infected?"

It sounded like Rose was on the verge of crying. No. 2 was shocked that Rose could sound like this, and it brought with it a sense of despair. Erica, Shion, and Gerbera were all silent. They had no expression and said no words. They just kept walking.

Gerbera, who had sighed and confessed about being a bullied child. Erica, who had said, her expression dark, that all she could remember from her childhood was battle. Shion, who had said she went through the same experience. It had hardly been an hour since that conversation.

"Just stop!" Sonia screamed as her knees buckled. The infected trio started to move differently. Their leisurely gaits turned into agile leaps. The three of them were scrambling for Sonia, guns and knives drawn.

"Watch out!"

She wanted to stop them but couldn't. There were now Machines engaging No. 2 and No. 4. Just a little while ago, it had been seven of them against one enemy. They didn't stand a chance then. Now there were only three of them, surrounded by enemies…

Rose wailed. Sonia screamed. No. 2 glanced at them while dodging the Machine barrage.

Rose stood in front of Sonia, impaled by a knife still gripped tightly by Gerbera. The wound was clearly mortal. The little girls shrieked in laughter.

"*The wound is deep.*"

"*You're done for.*"

Even still, Erica was heading for Rose and Sonia, knife in hand.

"Don't be…stupid!" Rose spat, as if she were coughing up blood. But that was it. No. 2 saw Sonia collapse.

"Big sis… Sorry…"

Erica's knife was tearing up Sonia's throat. Rose fell on her knees beside them.

"It's okay, Sonia." Rose embraced her.

"*And your actions were in vain.*"

"*Like we said, your sacrifices were meaningless.*"

Rose stood up. She was most likely using up every bit of her strength—her knees were buckling wildly.

"I found…a reason to live."

Rose slowly shuffled toward the girls.

"Do you two have a reason to…live?!"

Those were her last words. Rose succumbed before her sword could reach them.

"*Why do you fight?*"

"*Why do you want to die?*"

No. 2 felt murderous hatred toward the little girls. She wanted to slice them both open, slowly. This was the most animosity she'd ever felt toward a Mahcine.

"Shut up! Lowly extremities shouldn't be asking questions!"

No. 4 jumped into action before No. 2.

"*Can you beat us?*"

"*Why are you wasting your breath?*"

"*Why won't you give up?*"

"Shut up! Shut up! Shut up!"

No. 4 went berserk, swinging her sword wildly. She left herself open thanks to her raging attacks. It was the first time No. 2 had seen No. 4 so furious. No. 2 wanted to run in and act as support, but the Machines stalled her and kept her from doing so.

If only I were more powerful, thought No. 2. She wished she had the power to protect her comrades, from the bottom of her heart. But in reality she was painfully average—

No. 2 dodged the front legs and ran.

"No. 4, I'm coming! No. 4?"

No. 4 collapsed, all three of the infected androids bringing her down. No. 2 braced herself for them to attack her next, but it didn't happen. The little girls beckoned to the three, and they withdrew from No. 4. Even the Machine, which had been attacking constantly, scrambled back beside the little red girls.

Perhaps they wanted to give No. 4 time to say her goodbyes. Or they wanted to see No. 2 cry over the body of No. 4…

That didn't matter now. No. 2 ran to No. 4, and held her heavily wounded body.

"No. 4! Hold on!"

"Sorry No. 2… Was I…useless?"

"No you weren't! I was…I was the one…who dragged everybody into this."

No. 2 had suggested that they cooperate with the resistance. No. 16 had been against it, and No. 21 thought it wouldn't make a difference. No. 4 hadn't been supportive of the idea either. She must have agreed to it so No. 2 wouldn't have to operate solo.

If the four of them had gone on to attempt the mission, their success rate would have been zero. The four of them would have died anyway.

But Rose and the others—they wouldn't have had to die if they hadn't fought alongside the four of them.

Because I begged them to join forces with us…

"It was my fault. Now everyone's—"

"No, No. 2." No. 4 gripped No. 2's hand. Her hand felt so feeble. "We all chose to be here. Rose said so too, right? She found a…reason to live."

That's right. Rose's last words.

And…

"I want you to find a reason to live."

Those had also been Seed's last words. *A reason to live.*

At the time No. 2 didn't understand their meaning. Even now, she didn't. If everyone had a different reason to live, maybe it was normal for her not to know her own. But...

"But…!"

"Thanks for giving me a reason to live."

"No. 4…"

Perhaps No. 4 had used all her strength to talk, because her grip loosened. No. 2 firmly held on to her hand.

"Is this self-sacrifice?"

"Is this a story of self-sacrifice?"

"I want to laugh."

"It's funny."

The little red girls laughed. They were amused, after all. They were fascinated by what No. 4 would say with her dying breath, and how No. 2 would mourn her.

"This...this is..."

Her hand shook as it gripped her sword. No. 2 had to bite down to keep her anger from overflowing.

"Unforgivable..."

Right as she was about to rush the girls, No. 4 beat her to it again. Where she got the energy was a mystery, but she sprung up and swung her sword at the girls.

"Die!"

Just a little more. No. 4's sword stopped just before it hit the little girls, who were still laughing. Erica and the other two had stepped in to protect them.

The knife that originally wounded No. 4 slashed her yet again. No. 4 fell without a sound, a comrade who had covered for No. 2 right until the very end.

"Unforgivable—I won't forget this!"

No. 2 slashed at Shion. She too had been a comrade until the team breached the server room—until she had been possessed by the Machines and killed Sonia, Rose, and No. 4.

No. 2 split Shion's skull in half. She felt a delayed pang of pain in her chest.

"We're doing this because there's nothing we can do!"

No. 2 recalled what Dahlia had said. *So this is what she was talking about*, she thought in the back of her mind.

She turned and mowed Erica down. Her half-crushed head went flying through the air. It felt like pieces of her own body were being torn off and flung across the room.

She leapt on Gerbera, switching to a backhanded grip, and used the momentum from her fall. She stuck the sword in Gerbera's head, and pushed down. No. 2 felt something die inside of her.

Sorry, everyone…

She thought about when Anemone had pointed a gun at Lily. Rose had shouted, "Don't go near her!"

"*How horrible, it's so sad.*"

"*What a horrible child; it's so terrifying.*"

Their voices. So repulsive. This had all happened because of them.

"Shut up!"

Everyone had died because of them…

She reared back and swung her sword with all her might. Machines got in the way. She slammed them out of the way. Her sword sliced their bodies easily, as if all her struggles before had been a dream. In one motion, she hurled them away and sliced the girl on the right.

"What?"

She'd definitely made contact. The girls were grinning. No. 2 stuck her sword through the girl on the left. They kept grinning.

"Why…"

No matter how much she slashed or thrust her sword she felt no pressure or resistance on the sword's hilt, even though the little girls were definitely right there in front of her.

"*You can't kill us.*"

"*You can't kill us.*"

"Why?" she asked, her voice shivering. She couldn't tell whether that was from fear or anger.

"*My name is Terminal Alpha.*"

"*My name is Terminal Beta.*"

"*We are extremities.*"

"*We are manifestations of the network.*"

"*We are memories.*"

"*We are nothing more and nothing less.*"

No. 2 couldn't understand anything they said, but she realized now that a normal weapon would be ineffective. She looked around. If they were extremities, then they must actually exist in the server. If she destroyed the server room, wouldn't the two them also be destroyed as a consequence?

"Are you planning on destroying this place?"

"Just you alone?"

Perhaps they had read her mind, or she had betrayed her emotions with her expression. Either way, it made her uncomfortable that they had guessed right. She tightly grasped her sword.

"You don't know how many years that'll take, you know?"

"You'd need as much energy as a fusion reactor, you know?"

Then all she'd have to do would be to let her own internal fusion reactor explode. Like No. 16 had done.

"That's right. Your fusion reactor."

"That thing that's in it."

"That's right. If you scan it, you'll know."

"The bomb embedded within it."

No. 2 clutched unconsciously at her chest. She had noticed that something was off. That something had been attached to the fusion reactor inside of her. But she hadn't thought about it. It hadn't crossed her mind to investigate the object. She had been manipulated so she wouldn't think about it…

"When you all become nonfunctional in a certain location."

"That bomb will go off."

"The first condition is to arrive at the server room."

"The second condition is to be nonfunctional."

"When you all lose."

"We lose our victory as well."

The bomb had been embedded during manufacture. Command had overseen the manufacturing process. Which meant that…

"In conclusion, it was planned from the beginning."

"This battle plan assumed a losing scenario."

Now she knew why there were no reinforcements. If only one of them made it to this room, and then was killed, the server room would be destroyed.

"Don't androids laugh, in times like this?"

"Don't androids laugh, because they experience emotion?"

Their unpleasant laugh echoed around the room. She couldn't forgive them. She wanted to kill them. But that wasn't enough. That wasn't enough retribution for her fallen comrades…

It was then that No. 2 heard a noise behind her. Glancing back, she saw No. 4 stand up. At first she was afraid that she had been infected, but that wasn't the case.

"We're…durable. Because we're…new…models…"

No. 4 stood, taking labored breaths. Her footing was surprisingly stable, even though it was already incredible that she was still conscious.

"Go…No. 2. Leave this to me."

No. 4 grinned. Her outstretched arms approached No. 2. Contrary to her weakened hands from before, No. 4 forcefully shoved No. 2 to the ground.

"Don't! No. 4!"

No. 2 shrieked as she hit the ground. She needed to stop No. 4. If No. 4 died…if she was rendered nonfunctional in a certain location…

"No!"

A white explosion drowned out the little girls' laughs, and No. 2's scream.

[1209/08:00]

She couldn't tell what happened.

When No. 2 came to, she was buried in rubble. But she was still alive. She climbed out of the mess; she was dirty, and covered in cuts and bruises. She could feel her body complain with every breath.

She looked around. There was no trace of the server room. She was outside. The shape of Mount Ka'ala had changed. The explosion had apparently been colossal. She wasn't sure if the shock wave had blasted her away or if the mountain had collapsed and exposed the basement of the Machine complex. Either way, she had survived an explosion of this scale. It was a miracle.

Why me? she thought. She thought the same thing when they landed on Earth. But there was a definitive difference from then to now. At the time, she had thought, *It would've been better if somebody stronger than me survived.* Not this time.

It wouldn't have mattered who survived. Whether it had been the greatest leader, No. 1, or the android with the highest kill count, No. 3, the result would have been the same.

What determined who lived was not power or intelligence. It was sheer luck. Even so, she was chosen to live. A fate chosen on a whim. Then, she had to do whatever being a survivor entailed.

Destroy the Machines. Destroy everything. Nobody would get in her way. She would kill anybody who tried. Whoever that person would be.

"No. 4…"

No. 2 recalled No. 4's smile as she had left No. 2 with a simple "Bye." Command had planned the explosion that vaporized No. 4 without a trace.

No. 2 ripped off her goggles and slammed them on the ground. "That's against military regulations, you know?" She remembered No. 4's expression. And No. 16's reply, "Look who's talking!" And No. 21 saying, "Go on without me."

"Everyone…"

No. 2 ground the goggles under her heel. She didn't need them.

Machines approached, their movements jerky. Apparently, some were still active, even after the server was destroyed.

"You scraps…"

She scooped up some debris and flung it at the Machines, who quickly collapsed. It was effortless.

From somewhere, she heard a rumble. The explosion had probably caused many landslides to occur. She carefully started to walk along the landscape.

First, she had to escape this shitty place. After she repaired her chassis, she would go massacre the Machines. She would ruin them, one by one. That was her reason to live…

Glaring ahead, Attacker No. 2 drew her sword.

[11945 06 26]

She had had the dream many times. She fought with her comrades, heard her comrades scream…and she cried. She had it so often that she was aware it was a dream even while experiencing it.

"Good morning, A2."

But she hadn't expected to be called when she woke up. That was the only thing that was unusual.

"What?"

"YoRHa model A2 was rebooted 5 minutes and 42 seconds ago. Cause: Damage from an encounter with a large Machine."

The monotone voice from the floating box. Now she remembered. She engaged a large hostile in the desert, was exposed to an EMP attack, and lost consciousness right as the battle ended. She brushed sand off her and stood up.

"Shit! All this sand is annoying!"

"Report: Your fuel filter is damaged. It seems that particulates infiltrated your filter during battle. Recommendation: Swift replacement of the aforementioned part."

"Well it's easier said than done."

The box was always saying absurd things. She couldn't see how it was supposed to be a "support assistant."

"Records indicate that a filtration unit was recently active at the resistance camp."

She stared at the box in surprise. She hadn't misheard. It had definitely just said what she thought it said.

"Resistance camp…"

She knew that Anemone was alive. She had recently been told that information. Until then, she thought she had been the only survivor.

That day, after frantically escaping Mount Ka'ala, she removed the bomb in her. She threw away anything that seemed like it could contain location-sensing hardware and left behind almost all her equipment issued by Command. She wandered the Earth with just her long sword in hand. *Destroy as many Machines as possible.* That was the only thing on her mind.

She had died during that battle. Her old self was buried under the rubble with her comrades.

That's why even if she knew Anemone was alive, she didn't go out of her way to contact her. She didn't know what to do if she met her. But now she had a perfect excuse, in the form of a fuel filter, to go talk to her.

She peered toward the direction the box specified. She could see some high-rise structures beyond the sandstorms.

"Guess I'll go."

She walked, kicking sand as she went. She called out her comrades' names in her head. But she felt nothing.

She was empty inside.

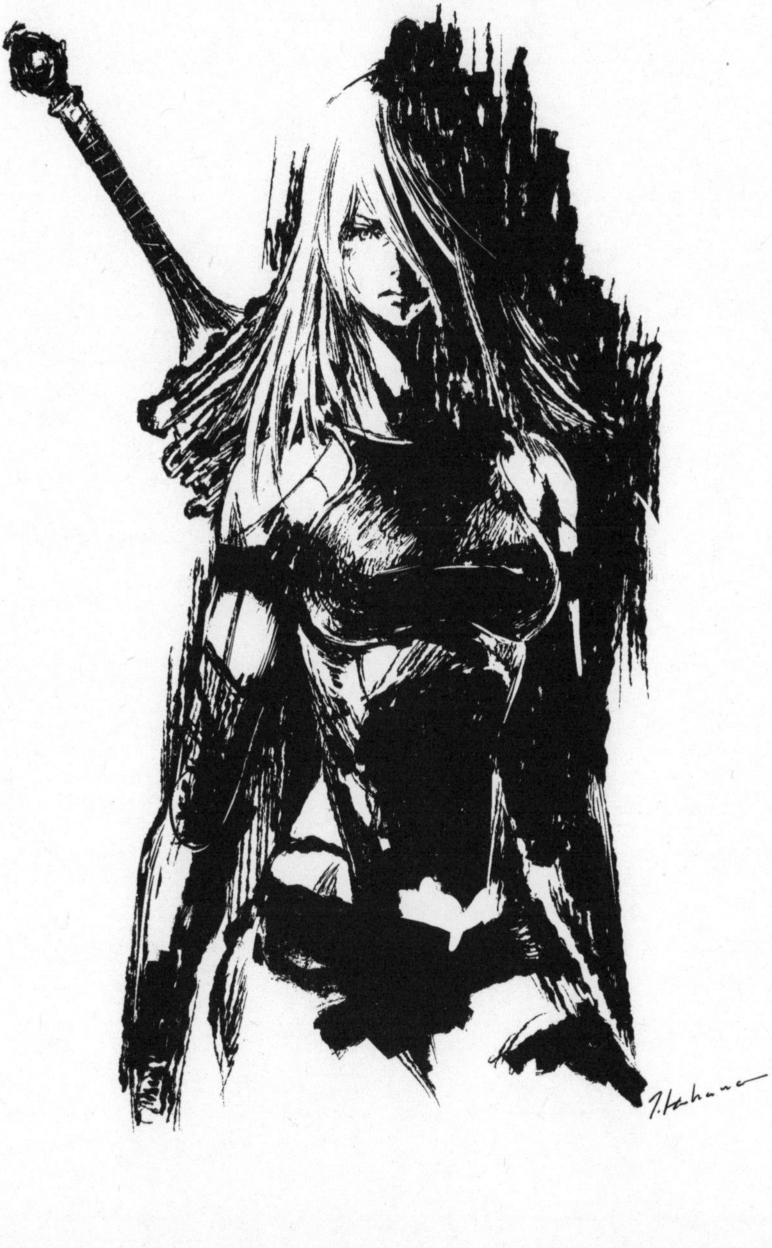

MEMORY CAGE

by Jun Eishima

THE CLOSE-COMBAT WEAPON FLASHED, SLICING THROUGH THE SANDSTORM. A Type-40 combat sword. A state-of-the-art weapon issued only to the elite forces on the front lines. The blade, crackling with electricity, burst and sent a semispherical object flying through the air in an arc.

A now-decapitated machine stopped moving. A few seconds later, it cylindrical body fell on its side in the sand, and explode, shrapnel showering two previously destroyed bodies in the vicinity.

After the explosion and shock wave, all that was left was the unique sound of the sirocco, the desert wind.

The dust eventually lifted, revealing a human silhouette. From the smooth outline of the shoulders, the tight waist, and alluring legs that emerged from a short skirt, the silhouette clearly belonged to an adult woman.

Though technically, the individual wasn't an adult, or a woman. The silhouette didn't belong to a human, or an organism with innate gender. It was YoRHa android Type B No. 2, code name 2B. A unit built for battle.

It had already been a long time since humans had left the Earth. Humanity was forced to flee to the moon because of the alien invasion. As of now, Earth was only occupied by the Machines, which were the aliens' minions, and the human-created androids, who were assigned to destroy the Machines.

2B sheathed her sword as she called out behind her.

"Was that all?"

Responding to her question, a support unit, called Pod, that had been floating several feet over her lowered itself closer to the ground.

It had a cuboid head with four variously sized arms. While it generally traveled through air, it could also propel itself through water. It had multifarious support functions, including long-range attacks, situational analysis, transmission capabilities, and emergency battlefield first aid.

"Affirmative: No enemy responses detected within a five-kilometer radius of the access point."

"I see," 2B mumbled as she approached a metal box slightly taller than she was. Access points were disguised as ancient human vending machines, but they were valuable apparatuses that enabled transmissions with Command and collected intel on their surroundings.

Whether they were aware of it or not, the Machines always gathered around these access points. Whether it be in the corner of a ruin or in the middle of a desert, without fail they collected around the vending machines as if they were insects swarming to a fallen fruit.

Inevitably, YoRHa squadron members needing to send a transmission or check the terrain data of the surroundings had to clear out the Machines around an access point. It was just standard operating procedure.

After completing this step 2B could finally attend to her original errand. She opened her mail inbox on the display, and retrieved a newly received email. She read the sender, the classification of top secret, and some of the message, when—

"2B!"

Suddenly appearing out of nowhere was Type S No. 9, a.k.a. 9S. While he was a YoRHa android, he wasn't modeled after an adult woman like 2B, but instead a teenage boy.

"Is that mail from Command?"

It wasn't as though he had looked, but scanner types like him that specialized in research had exceptional observational skills and intuition. It wasn't time for the regular report from the human board on the moon to come, and she surely wouldn't have engaged many Machines just to open a personal message. He had probably taken those factors into account, and instantaneously arrived at the conclusion that it was mail from Command.

"It has nothing to do with this research mission. It's some directives for another mission."

"Anyway," 2B changed the subject. "This isn't the rendezvous point."

The assigned rendezvous point with 9S was closer to their mission destination.

"I know, but it seemed like you were in battle, so I thought I'd come in as support."

"No need to worry about me."

If she hadn't been able to take care of those Machines, she would be a dysfunctional Type B.

"I guess." 9S dropped his shoulders with an exaggerated motion. "Well, since we were able to meet up, let's continue on together."

After consulting their map data, 2B and 9S started to head toward their mission destination.

"Ugh. More sand got in."

It would have been remarkable had water gotten into their shoes as they walked the desert. But sand was to be expected, and 2B thought it was nothing to make a fuss about. On the other hand, 9S would scowl every few meters, walk a short distance, groan in frustration, and go through the same cycle over and over.

"Doesn't it bother you, 2B?"

"What?"

"Aren't your shoes full of sand as well?"

"While it's uncomfortable, it doesn't disturb my walking, so…"

Sandstorms in the air obstructed vision, but sand in their shoes was no problem. "Just don't worry about it," said 2B, at which 9S dropped his shoulders yet again.

"Having sand in your shoes feels disgusting, doesn't it? It doesn't disturb my walking, but it's a matter of sanity."

"We are prohibited from experiencing emotion."

How many times had she said the same thing to 9S? This wasn't the first time she had gone on a mission with him.

"Roger."

9S's reply was the same every time, made with a slightly sour tone and expression. Well, of course the first time he had been apologetic and said "Sorry," but still.

She had heard that YoRHa androids were prohibited from experiencing emotion ever since a squadron member had jeopardized a mission because of them. Indeed, emotion impaired judgment and action. 2B thought that emotion was unnecessary for androids.

Especially for herself.

"Oh! Is that it?"

Ahead, in the direction 9S was pointing, a building jutted out of the horizon. The building had been displayed on the map data all along, but the topological variation of the terrain and sandstorms had concealed it until now.

"Affirmative: The main subject of this research mission. A massive building, remnant of human civilization."

Pod answered from the side. It wasn't 2B's particular model, Pod 042, but 9S's, Pod 153. A Pod would usually only interact with its support targets, unless it was specifically called upon or in a tough situation.

The wind suddenly weakened, and the field of vision became clear. They could see an arched entrance on the face of the building. They could tell that the building was dug into a mountain. But looking at the map data, not all of the building was built into the mountain. Some parts of it faced out into the valley. Overall, it was built very strangely.

"It was apparently a religious facility called a temple. Its official name was 'The Sand Temple,' I think? Humans used to live here a long time ago, and after that it was used as a temple...I heard."

Perhaps she was imagining things, but 9S sounded excited. Since the role of Type S was to perform research and gather data, they had the trait of being exceptionally curious.

"Let's get going, 2B," 9S said impatiently, and started running as he kicked up sand. That must've gotten more sand in his shoes than before, but he didn't seem to care. It had evidently been a matter of mind. 2B felt a smile creeping onto her lips, and quickly suppressed the urge.

"Emotion is prohibited…"

She had planned to say it internally, but ended up accidentally saying it out loud.

9S looked back and shouted, "Did you say something?!"

"Nothing," 2B answered, as she hurried toward the the Sand Temple.

■　■■

There's no sound, she thought. That's how quiet the interior of the temple was. She realized with a delay that it was because the thick walls of the temple blocked out the sound of the desert winds, which outside still persisted.

"I didn't expect this place to have air conditioning!"

Pod 153 responded to 9S. "Negative: There is no air-conditioning unit near the entrance of the building. The body is perceiving a lower temperature because of the temperature differential between the desert and the interior of the building."

"Boo. It feels like it." 9S sulked as he trotted along the hallway. 2B was wary of the surroundings as she followed.

Their footsteps and the low humming of the Pods overlapped. A part of the ceiling had collapsed, and rays of natural light poured down. The light let them see the stairs and floor, which was packed with rows of square blocks of stone.

"There's even sand in the building."

9S put his hand on the stair railing and looked down over it. The stairway was completely coated with sand. Sand not only filled the hallways, but there were small piles of sand next to the walls as well.

"Hypothesis: The sand in the hallways and near the walls was intentionally circulated by humans. However, the date of occurrence and motive are unknown."

"Intentionally circulated? You mean they poured the sand into the temple? Like a river?"

"Affirmative: For convenience sake, we will call it artificial quicksand."

"Why would they do something like that? Oh, did you say the motive was unknown?"

"Affirmative."

There were many mysteries from ancient civilization. While humans had fled to the moon, they hadn't taken all their belongings. That's why androids performed research and kept records.

"Are there any Machines nearby?"

She didn't see any enemy responses on her goggles, but 2B asked Pod 042 just in case. It was better to be safe than sorry.

"Answer: There is no enemy presence in the temple."

That meant that even if 9S, a ball of curiosity, did something sporadic, they wouldn't be in immediate danger. Of course, there were some Machines that could jam their sensors, so they weren't completely off the hook.

"Warning: The stairs and a part of the floor ahead are damaged."

9S laughed in response to 153's warning. "I know. You don't have to tell me. Right 2B?"

2B nodded.

She could see a huge boulder blocking the descending staircase by the entrance.

"This boulder used to be a part of the ceiling. The surface is worn down, but I can see some patterns on it." 9S, who was kneeling on one knee inspecting the boulder, glanced up at the ceiling. Seeing that, 2B also looked up. She could see the sky through a gaping hole.

"I wonder why it collapsed…"

At the very least, it wasn't the aftermath of a Machine battle. The androids were created to return Earth to its rightful human owners. So when they fought, they tried to use methods that wouldn't put human artifacts in danger.

That's why it was hard to believe that a battle would take place so close to such a large artifact as this building. If, hypothetically, androids had encountered Machines, they would have lured them to a different place before engaging in battle.

"Answer: The collapse is estimated to have happened thousands of years ago. Therefore, the cause is indeterminate."

"Thousands of years ago, huh. Amazing."

"Amazing?"

"Well, if the ceiling collapsed thousands of years ago, that must mean this temple was built even earlier than that? It's amazing that this building is in such good condition. Since the desert winds are so harsh, I would've expected more erosion to take place, especially for a stone structure like this." 9S, who had said all of that in one breath, suddenly stood up. As if he were being sucked in, he quickly headed toward the room next to the staircase.

"What next?" 2B asked, a little irritated. 9S was inspecting the open door.

"I wonder how they opened and closed this door. It's stone, you know? This thickness and size. It's not something humans would be able to easily move."

The sliding door consisted of two panels, but neither would budge no matter how much they pushed or pulled. 9S tilted his head to the side as he stared at the partition.

"Maybe there's a power source somewhere?"

9S peered inside the room. But in contrast to the hallway, which was lit by natural light from above, the room was pitch-black and seemed to extend forever. Pod 153 blocked 9S as he attempted to enter the dark room.

"Recommendation: Illumination area."

"Okay, that's perfect."

"Roger."

What lay illuminated in 153's light was surprisingly a large space. 9S ran after 153 toward the middle of the room. The entrance grew dark again. After instructing 042 to illuminate the way, 2B also stepped into the room.

9S inspected the ceiling and the walls. As he moved, his shoes made squeaks that echoed throughout the room. Then he suddenly crouched down to inspect the tiles on the floor. Just watching 9S made 2B dizzy.

"The floor, walls, and ceiling were all made by stacking stones. They cut them uniformly, laid them out—this architectural style is different from any other one I've seen. I wonder what kind of equipment they used? How did they carry that much heavy material? How does such a thin pillar support a room this tall and wide?"

9S rushed toward a portion of the wall, talking with fascination in his voice. "Did there used to be a light here? On this thin table?"

"Affirmative: There is evidence that torches, a type of illumination, used to be placed here."

One, two, three, four—there's eight of them. I wonder what they used this room for? It doesn't seem like it served a ritualistic purpose."

After running around excessively, 9S headed toward a door in the back. The door at the entrance was open, but this door was closed.

"I doubt it but…" 9S placed his hand on the handle. "What if this door easily opens—yeah right," 9S said, drowned out by a creaking sound. The door slid open from both sides.

"It opened?"

9S looked surprised as he looked at the open door. Pod 153 kept the light on as it went in through the door and then came back. Checking the surroundings for any danger was also a duty of a support unit.

"Warning: The hallway is significantly below the door's height."

But 153's warning could not deter the Type S's curiosity.

"I'm going to go look a little. I'll be back right away!"

After 9S let go, the door closed behind him.

2B sighed after 9S and 153 disappeared from sight. This was her chance.

"Pod program, activate close-combat support and weaponry."

"Roger: Electronic signal camouflage activated, close-combat attacks activated."

Pod 042 went through the procedures.

"Combat mode changed to anti-YoRHa. Personal identification signal erased."

Her heart was heavy as she thought of what she had to do. In order to settle herself down, 2B stood still as she drew her sword.

It was part of her assignment. It was a mission, in the category of top secret. She'd received a notification for new mail right after she exited her flight unit. Not on the Bunker in orbit, or after they had entered the stratosphere. Pod 042 notified her right as they landed in the desert.

She knew right away what the subject matter was. A message directly from the commander, not sent through an operator. Sent when it was least likely to be intercepted. Above top secret.

No. She knew far before she received the message. She knew when she was assigned to a human civilization research mission with 9S. She was sure she would have to assassinate 9S in the near future. Her prediction had unfortunately now come true.

"Pod. Give me 9S's location and a route to approach him through this hallway."

"Roger: 9S's black box response targeted, calculating best route."

2B stood with her back to the door that 9S and 153 had gone through. It was better to hunt him using a different route. It would be easier to run into him than chase him.

Furthermore, the target was a Type S, a new model that specialized in research and data collection. She had to be cautious, or else she might lose the element of surprise.

Of course, she had much higher battle capabilities. The result would be the same, regardless of whether or not she surprised him. But she wanted to be done with her task as quick as possible, before 9S realized he was being attacked. That way she could spare him some fear and pain…

"Calculation complete," 042 said, as 2B retraced her steps through the hallway she had passed. She leapt onto the boulder that was blocking the staircase, and jumped. 9S's black box response was much closer now.

This time she carefully crept down the stairs, trying not to make a sound. The black box response was coming from the next room. She quietly drew her sword and approached the door.

Just like the first room, these double doors were wide open as well. But she couldn't see 9S.

She got closer to the door, and quickly scanned around. The room was empty. Which meant there was nowhere to hide as well. She wondered if she should enter…

2B felt a presence behind her. She quickly dove to the side and evaded a shower of bullets that rained down right where she had been standing. She recognized it as a long-range attack from a Pod program.

She tried to right herself, but saw a blade coming toward her. 9S had come up behind her and was swinging his close-combat long sword.

2B didn't expect to be attacked by 9S himself. To think she'd tried to ambush him, but had been ambushed herself.

Right as she was about to kick 9S's sword hand, she realized something.

Why was 9S holding his close-combat weapon? 9S never gripped his sword by the handle like this…

She quickly created some distance between them. She saw the sword, now molten, leave drippings like wax on the ground. Had she kicked his hand a moment ago, her right leg would have suffered a lot of damage. 9S must have predicted what a Type B close-combat specialist would do in that situation, and set a trap for her.

It was better to go elsewhere. She was at a disadvantage in the hallway, because she'd come in after 9S and didn't know what lay ahead.

Taking a big leap backward, she created even more distance between her and 9S and jumped through a door. This was another room, not the one in which 9S's black box response was detected. He probably wouldn't have had the time to set a trap in this room.

9S chased after 2B. There was nowhere to hide, but 9S went after her with no hesitation. Pod 153 fired long-range attacks while he attacked from close range. 2B was shocked at 9S's relentless style of fighting. She had never seen him like this.

Dodging 153's gunfire and heat beams, 2B swung her sword at 9S. But 9S was more nimble than she had expected, and she couldn't deal a decisive blow. No, it was Pod's long-range attacks that were hindering her. She needed to deal with 153 somehow, so she called out to 042. "Pod! Set your attack target to 153!"

Support units had no "relentless attack" mode. If they were dealt damage, they always chose to evade further attacks, which meant that 153 would temporarily suspend long-range attacks while it was evading. It gave 2B one or two seconds, which was enough.

The barrage of gunshots paused for a moment. 2B immediately closed the distance between her and 9S. Perhaps he had not expected 153 to be attacked, because he just stood still. She pointed her sword at 9S and stepped forward. Just when she thought it was over, she felt a bad feeling run through her body. Her sword dropped from her hands.

2B's eyes widened in surprise—or they tried to, but couldn't even muster that. Her arms, legs, and the rest of her body were all unresponsive.

She could see the floor tiling approaching her. No, she was just falling forward. Right before she hit the ground, she heard 9S say, "I'm sorry."

"So it wasn't just me," 9S mumbled. But it wasn't vocalized. In the hacking dimension "talking" was just recorded on 9S's personal data. The white walls and floor were also only things that 9S's personal data perceived, since they didn't actually exist.

He'd hoped it wasn't true. That 2B was plotting to kill him. But he saw evidence in her word selection, fleeting expressions, and her tone that supported his suspicion. Eventually that suspicion turned into certainty, and certainty into reality.

"I didn't really want to do this…"

It wasn't a lie. He was telling the truth. He just couldn't think of any other way. He had tried to think of an alternative ever since he realized that 2B was an overseer sent by Command. But he couldn't think of a realistic plan.

"But a Type S could never beat a Type B."

He was well aware of 2B's battle capabilities, given all the times they had been assigned together. If he couldn't hack her chassis and take control, he would be killed without a doubt.

Since 2B rarely let her guard down, he had to wait for the moment 2B would finish him off in a close-combat battle. A predator was most vulnerable when it was capturing its prey. It was something 9S had learned by observing the animals on Earth.

On the other hand, his plan only worked because 2B was seriously trying to kill him. If she hadn't intended on killing him, she would not have been provoked into entering hacking range, no matter the ferocity of 9S's attacks. The fact that 9S was still alive was proof of 2B's murderous intent.

"Either way, it's a bad excuse isn't it?"

He knew that he was doing something worse than murder. He was infiltrating 2B's mind, rummaging through it, and on top of that planned to kill her afterward. He knew. But still.

"There's something I needed to know."

9S carefully proceeded through 2B's memory block. He hadn't hacked her just to take control of her chassis and kill her. He wanted some information.

"As such, we order you to assassinate 9S."

One of the newer memories in the memory block was something that looked like part of an email. It was most likely the mail she had received previously at the access point. Incomplete memories were stored in order of impact, instead of being stored sequentially.

When 2B had opened the email, the words "As such, we order you to assassinate 9S." were the first words she saw. Which meant that 2B had expected to receive the order. She must've read those words first, because she had been expecting them all along.

"We have evidence"

"Attempted to"

"The subject matter,"

"Access the main server"

"An unresolved problem for some time"

"Several times"

"It is prohibited"

"9S is"

The shards of the memory were all over the place. The order of the words was out of place, because 2B had been rattled by the message. Furthermore, 9S had appeared while she was reading it. She hadn't had time to organize all the information in the message…

9S moved further into the memory block, looking for the information he needed.

"Is this it? A confidential meeting between 2B and the commander."

It consisted of the commander standing with her back to 2B, as 2B looked on. Apparently this didn't take place through a transmission, but somewhere within the Bunker.

"But isn't a Type S on-site research mission usually completed solo?"

"It's just a formality. There can be exceptions. What if the area is infested with large numbers of Machines? There needs to be someone to support the Type S, who's unsuited for battle."

"Roger that. Then I'll proceed as you wish."

"For now, just supervision is fine. I'll tell you what further actions to take later."

This was a memory from before 2B started accompanying 9S on his missions. But at this point, he shouldn't have done anything "prohibited." But the commander thought supervision was necessary. Why?

Then, all of a sudden, another memory concerning 9S interrupted this one.

"For us scanner types, solo missions are the norm. That's why I think it's really exciting to have someone with me."

Ah, he remembered this. He had said this on their first mission together. 2B had probably thought about the meeting as he was talking to her then.

Back then, he hadn't realized 2B was supervising him, let alone known that there would be "further actions" taken against him.

Brushing his bitter feelings aside, he moved on to the next memory. It seemed like it was a transmission, and he heard the commander's voice with static mixed in.

"…Type S's are specialized in research and data collection. Because of their proficiency, they always end up knowing too much. I guess you could say it's fate for a Type S…"

What's wrong with knowing too much? 9S thought. Was there something Command needed to hide?

"9S will eventually commit a prohibited action. Perhaps he's already crossed the line."

He couldn't disagree with this. He had attempted to access the prohibited main server.

"There's no evidence yet. But it seems like there was an unauthorized attempt to access the server. This time whoever it was failed, but next time…"

That was right, he had failed at first. He'd fled from an aggressive firewall. He had escaped quickly, so he shouldn't have left any traces. The next time he gave up after passing one firewall. The next time he passed several firewalls. The more firewalls he passed, the more time it took for him to escape. There was greater risk of getting caught.

It might have been only a matter of time before he was caught. But he still wanted to know. The closer he got, the more he wanted it. If there was something he didn't know, he *had* to know.

Indeed, this was a Type S's fate. The commander was right in saying that, and continuing to supervise him. Even her order to assassinate him might've been justified.

The next memory was of yet another room of the Bunker. This time it captured the commander from the front, rather than the back.

"Type S's are unsuited for battle. I doubt I'll have trouble dealing with him."

"They are unsuited for close combat, but it's not like they can't fight. And Type S's are sharp. There's a high possibility that he's already aware that Command has sent someone to supervise him."

"It doesn't seem that he's aware…"

"You aren't suited for observation. Just like how Type S's are unsuited for battle."

The commander was also correct here. 2B hadn't realized that 9S knew about her real role.

At first, he thought 2B was just pretending not to have realized. But that doubt soon escaped him. 2B was not that shrewd. In fact, she was quite inept. The glimpses of kindness and concern—maybe 2B thought she was hiding them well, but they were easy for a Type S to discern.

"Either way, if we attack him, 9S will undoubtedly counterattack. Using hacking, which is a Type S's specialty."

How sharp. 9S wanted to applaud her. The commander's prediction had come precisely true.

Now he had half of his answers. 2B needed to kill him because he knew too much. Now, where could he find the other half?

"Let 9S go ahead and activate my weaponry then. I'll try to ambush him when we run into each other."

A random memory shard interrupted the conversation between the commander and 2B.

"If it's over quickly…"

This was clearly an older memory compared to the conversation. 2B had been thinking of how to kill 9S long before the order came to do so.

"Don't let 9S realize what happened to him… That way, I'll spare him some fear and pain."

Now he had all the answers. *I see*, he thought, as the random memory disappeared.

"Even you, a close-combat specialist, would not stand a chance if 9S hacked and took control of your chassis. That's why."

What? What did she make 2B do? The ambush was not an order from the commander. What did the commander make her do?

"I want you to set a trap in the hacking dimension."

He felt uneasy. Suddenly, black walls appeared in the previously white hacking dimension. Orange and purple balls of light chased 9S as he turned. It was a trap-style logic virus.

They could effectively attack 9S's personal data if they set up some viruses in the memory block. However, the virus would affect 2B as well. 9S hadn't expected them to go this far.

"Shit! I underestimated them!"

It had been more of a desire for 9S, not a prediction. The commander had mercilessly chosen to put 2B in danger.

He needed to escape before his personal data was infected.

"But logic virus attacks might not be enough. That's why we're going to set one more trap."

Where was the escape route?! He had made sure there was a way out?!

"We'll block everything off, and trap him in the logic circuit."

All of a sudden he couldn't move. Spheres kept multiplying within the dimension. It was a firewall created by a self-shutdown algorithm.

"Pod! Create a new escape route!"

But Pod did not reply. Not only had the logic virus attacked 9S's personal data, it had also cut off any communication with the outside world.

His escape route was gone. In a few seconds his current personal data would be purged and cease to exist. 9S looked on as the white hacking dimension's environment became a sea of black.

"I guess it's over..."

2B had received the assassination order at the desert access point. Since then, she'd had countless chances to assassinate 9S. The desert, which had no places to hide and bad footing, put 2B at an advantage. But 2B didn't make her move until they were inside the temple. Looking inside her memories, he understood why. 2B was very adept after all.

It was to end it as quickly as possible, so 9S could die without realizing what had happened.

The spheres filled in his surroundings. But he strangely felt at peace. He didn't feel fear or pain.

"Bye, 2B."

Then, darkness overtook him.

Control of her body came back just as fast as it had been taken from her.

"Self-shutdown activated. Logic circuit blocked off. Quarantined."

After blinking a few times to check for control of her body, she slowly sat up. There were no problems with her motor capabilities either.

"...Delete."

She hadn't felt anything, not even a slight pain, like the prick of a needle. She just knew that the command had been executed.

She looked down at her side, at the chassis of 9S. While his black box response was still active, deleting his personal data had left his chassis nonfunctional.

It would have been fine had she finished him off in combat; even if she failed to do so the rigged logic virus would attack his personal data. Even if 9S succeeded in eliminating the logic virus, the self-shutdown sequence would trap him in the logic circuit. Then the whole circuit could be disposed of. The whole ploy had been constructed by the commander.

9S had thought two steps ahead by hacking 2B after close combat, but the commander had thought three steps ahead. It was her win.

2B held her sword with a backhand grip, and swung once.

"Head destroyed."

She felt a strange sensation in her arm. She had never experienced this before. Even though this wasn't the first time she had killed a comrade, she had never felt something like this when she had "relieved" her comrades on the battlefield countless times before. Was her assassination not thorough enough?

"Chest destroyed."

She thrust her sword one more time. This was strange. The sensation was spreading. At first it had only affected her arm. Now the pressure had spread to her whole upper body. She wasn't being physically suppressed. But it was hard for her to breathe.

"Black box response confirmed to be unresponsive."

She had completely destroyed the chassis. His personal data was erased as well. 9S was dead. Her task was complete. But she felt like she had missed something. A nagging feeling of helplessness. Perhaps her breathing mechanism was experiencing some sort of issue.

"Bye 2B."

She replayed 9S's parting words in her head. His last words, stored in her memories. She realized what had been bothering her, what had been nagging at her in the back of her mind.

"I see. So this is…"

It was an emotion called guilt. Or perhaps self-condemnation. Either way, emotions were prohibited.

Something resurfaced when she tried to kill her emotions. They were memories of 9S.

"2B," he called. "It's exciting to operate alongside someone else," She remembered the bashful smile as he had told her that. What mission

was that, when he sounded irritated and had said, "2B, you can be surprisingly careless sometimes…"

She felt a lump in the back of her throat. She felt her chest tighten
like she was being strangled. She just kept gritting her teeth. She understood for the first time what it felt like for the living to be tormented by
memories of the dead.

This was her fault. She had accumulated more memories than was
necessary…

"Bye, 2B."

Again. The same voice, again.

She vigorously shook her head and brushed away 9S's thoughts.

"I won't apologize."

It was a mission. She had no guilt. Never. If she got the same order,
she would do it again.

That's my job, she told herself, and raised her head.

"Pod, a transmission to Command."

"Roger."

Pod brought up the transmission display.

She was going to do the same thing again, that was for sure. But the
next time she was going to keep unnecessary interactions to a minimum.

She was going to minimize their time spent together, and their conversations, so she wouldn't accumulate unnecessary memories. So she
wouldn't have any prohibited emotions.

"This is Command."

She took a deep breath one more time, and exhaled, clearing her
chest of all the pain.

"This is 2B. The mission is complete."

Traces of something like grains of sand were sprinkled in her otherwise indifferent tone.

ORBITAL BUNKER OBSERVATION DIARY

by Jun Eishima

<Where 1s th1s?>
<Wh0 1s th1s?>

[TB13:30]

It's like I'm climbing a mountain of boulders, thought 2B.

Her left leg felt heavier than lead, and stepping forward made her breathe heavily. When she finally put her left foot forward, her right leg joints complained with a loud creak.

She half-rolled out of the flight unit, left the hangar, and stumbled a few meters into the hallway. The time it took to do all that was appalling. The Research and Development department was just past the hallway. Thinking of how long it would take made her dizzy.

The orbital Bunker was a camp for the YoRHa squadron on the front lines. It carried all the equipment and facilities necessary to deploy troops to Earth, and contained living quarters, but it wasn't grand by any meaning of the word. Yet she felt like her destination was eons away. The hallway had a gentle slope so there were no steps along the way. Someone could walk through with their eyes closed.

Put simply, the damage to her motor capabilities was grave. She desperately needed to have R&D recalibrate her, and attempted to quicken her steps.

The commander approached her from ahead. She tried to use her left arm to salute her, but she wasn't able to raise the limb all the way. 2B scowled. Apparently it wasn't just her legs that were damaged.

"Ah, make yourself comfortable."

The commander had probably deduced 2B's condition from her awkward salute. She made a motion for 2B to put her arm down.

"Your condition seems pretty bad."

"Since I wasn't able to get repairs on Earth, I was forced to come back here. I'm terribly sorry."

"No, you don't have to apologize. Were there any other wounded?"

"Due to a battle with Machines that appeared at dawn today, 1D's upper right arm as well as her right shoulder and 4B's left thigh sustained light injuries. Both were able to recover, due to 12H's efforts, to the point where they would not hinder to the mission."

"I see."

The commander averted her eyes to the side. This hallway, which connected the hangar to the R&D department and command room, faced "outside"—that is, outer space. They could see a black expanse dotted with stars, as well as Earth, the erstwhile home of the human race.

On that blue, beautiful planet, androids led by the YoRHa squadron were in a constant battle with Machines. No matter how many times they were crushed, the Machines kept spawning like the litter critters they were.

"Compared to enemy forces the YoRHa squadron is lacking in personnel, even though we pass it off nicely as a group of the select few."

Up until now, they had made up for the obvious disparity in numbers by using strategy and skill. But it wasn't enough to completely erase their disadvantage, and the battle had become drawn out. That's why 2B expected the commander to tell her to work harder, but she was wrong.

"So, don't force yourself, all right?" The commander smiled. At times, the commander would smile so gently it stumped 2B, even though her orders were as strict as any military leader's and her decision-making was as cool and collected as a freshly sharpened knife.

Behind this occasional smile, there was most likely an immeasurable amount of struggle and conflict.

"Commander…" she started, and stopped. *That's my problem*, 2B thought to herself. "No, never mind."

The commander's smile disappeared. Her lips strung together a few quiet words.

"No matter how harsh, we need to finish our job. The YoRHa squadron, that is."

The YoRHa squadron, 2B repeated in her mind. She had struggled in the past. She had felt unbearable pain...that was certain. But she'd never complained about a mission.

"But whatever mission that may be, the responsibility falls to me. Don't forget that," Commander said.

It was as if the commander had read her mind. 2B had thought that the baggage she accumulated after each and every mission was something she needed to shoulder herself. No, she still thought that way. But the commander's words resonated with her.

"Glory to humans." This time, 2B could properly place her left arm over her chest.

"Glory to humans," the commander repeated. She would fight under this person. In the future as well. Until they could return Earth to humans.

Listening to the orderly footsteps that receded farther and farther behind her, 2B hurried to the R&D department.

<What was that?>
<What was that, just n0w?>
<Sh0uld we f0ll0w?>
<Let's f0ll0w!>

[TB13:40]

From the moment she entered the command room, the commander was surrounded. A few operators had run toward her and blocked the path.

"Commander! It's about the Bunker's material storage—"

"Please allow me to report about the battle taking place in the City Ruins."

"Please approve the materials we're sending to the moon."

"There seem to be some technical problems with the transmission area in the third ward of the F sector."

Apparently the operators thought that just being the commander boosted her processing power.

"For the materials, talk to the representative of each and narrow down the storage plans to three options. Give them to me and I'll discuss it with you."

"Roger that."

"I'll listen to the battle status in 330 seconds."

"Roger that."

"I approve the materials."

"Thank you."

"Have all members in the F sector visit the access point, and investigate what's wrong."

"Roger."

Phew, that's all of them… Or so she thought, but the operators didn't budge. It seemed like they still had something on their minds.

"And?"

"Yes," the operators replied in unison.

"Commander! Please accept this!"

She was suddenly surrounded by outstretched packages, some of them gold and some of them silver.

"What? What's this?"

"Today is February 14. It's called Valentine's Day, and you're supposed to give brown things to people you respect."

"Valentine's? Is it an ancient tradition?"

"Yes! Apparently both the giver and receiver were able to experience happiness. The brown things were often wrapped in gold or silver paper."

Figures, she thought. While the shape and size varied, all the packages were sparkling. So humans handed each other such things in ancient times.

She opened one of the packages. It was a brown ribbon. *What am I supposed to do with this?* was her first thought, but she said thank you anyway.

There were many mysterious ancient traditions. Since humans created the androids, it was disrespectful to even try to understand their traditions, and mimicking an action without understanding wasn't very commendable. Mimicking this "Valentine's" tradition was something she shouldn't allow as a superior, but…

But I probably shouldn't be so strict, she thought to herself. Operators faced a different kind of struggle than the members that fought on the front lines.

"Commander, um…is now a good time?"

It was Operator 6O, who managed communications with 2B.

"What is it?"

"I'd like your approval to test the new flight unit equipment in the field."

She had been getting updates about the new equipment from the R&D department. If they were going to test it in the field, there would need to be communication between the operators and squadron members. Operator 6O had been in charge of those matters.

"Ah yes, that. For the recon mission. The person that was assigned to that was—"

"9S. If there's no problem with the recon mission, it'll be the last test involving the descent squadron."

Hearing that, the commander suddenly thought of 2B's expression from earlier.

"I see, 9S…that's right."

All the responsibility falls to me. She told herself the line she had said over and over in the past.

"Roger."

"Thank you very much."

Operator 6O bowed and left the command room. "Okay," the commander said as she turned around. That was exactly 330 seconds.

"Let me hear the battle status."

<Battles 0n Earth? Battle status?>
<Fighting 0n Earth? 1sn't that about how the battles are g0ing?>
<I see. I w0nder what they mean by new equ1pment.>
<I d0n't kn0w.>
<Sh0uld we g0 see?>
<Let's g0 see.>

[TB14:00]

Operator 6O rushed to the hangar. She didn't want to miss her. Though, even if she missed her, all she had to do was send a transmission.

She squeezed her body through the partially opened door. The door opened at a dreadfully slow speed. Swift action required responsive equipment, and she made a mental note to request faster doors later.

"21O, are you here?"

Operator 21O popped her head out from beneath a flight unit that was locked into the catapult. She was in the middle of a checkup. It was good timing. Operator 6O went straight to the point.

"In-field testing of the new equipment got approved!"

But 21O looked confused. Did she forget about the experiment?

"The new equipment? For the flight unit!"

Operator 21O, whose eyebrows were furrowed in confusion, suddenly looked irritated.

"Is that all?"

"What do you mean, is that all…?"

This time it was 6O that looked puzzled. What was 21O so irritated about?

"Something like that, you could have just used a transmission. There was no reason for you to come here."

"That's true, but…" 6O searched for an excuse to satisfy the disgruntled 21O. "But, but! I'm always using transmissions, so I needed some exercise!"

One of 21O's eyebrows moved. *So what*, her expression said.

"And don't you think it's important to do final equipment checks visually? Um, you know. We are? Prepared? What was the line?"

"Being prepared for anything is our job as operators."

"Yeah!"

21O finally shook her head after hearing 6O's enthusiastic outburst.

"You're probably right. We don't know what he'll do with new equipment. 9S is a ball of curiosity after all."

Contrary to how 21O said this with her shoulders shrugged, her tone was caring. She was always like this when she talked about 9S, the unit she supported.

"You're right," 6O said as she bent over. Although their support units were different, she could agree as a fellow operator.

"Ms. 2B is also a troublemaker sometimes."

Just like how Type S's were governed by their curiosity, Type B's were troublesome because they never hesitated to sacrifice themselves. That's probably why they were able to fight on the front lines, in the midst of whizzing bullets.

"I get nervous just watching."

"Even though I know it's because of our personality traits."

"I wouldn't mind if she was just a bit more prudent."

"But even if we tell her, would it make a difference?"

"There's nothing we can do!"

"That's why," Operator 6O and 21O said together, "it's vital to be prepared!"

And it was also vital for the operators to exchange information. Even a casual conversation was a form of information exchange. The trivial amounts of data could one day accumulate into something that dictated a big decision, or an indication of coming danger. In other words, every aspect of an operator's life was relevant to their job. They lived for their job.

6O and 21O checked the new and important features of the equipment, and talked for a little while. Of course, 21O never stopped working.

"Okay, sorry for the wait."

21O finished her inspection, and returned the flight unit to its designated space, making way for 6O. Since the catapult could hold only one flight unit at a time, they also had to carry out their inspections one at a time.

"Well, I'll contact 9S then."

"All right. Thanks!"

6O positioned the flight unit in the open space, and began her inspection.

<That mach1ne is b1g, 1sn't 1t?>

<1s that the new equ1pment?>

<Where sh0uld we g0 next?>

[TB14:30]

It was easy for Operator 21O to determine 9S's location.

On Earth, there were times that his location could not be determined due to the orbital video resolution or bad transmission conditions. But on the Bunker, she always knew where he would be. *9S must be here*, she thought as she arrived at the door.

The server maintenance room. It was the room with the Bunker's main terminal. 9S was always here, analyzing enemy defenses and studying new hacking patterns. 9S loved that kind of meticulous work.

Unless he was deployed, he was always, always, always in here doing work. His focus was so intense that he often could not hear the door open behind him.

See, just what I expected, 21O affirmed in her head. 9S was intently staring at the terminal, and hadn't noticed 21O enter the room. They were hidden behind the goggles, but his eyes were probably twinkling with fascination while he was immersed in his work.

Apparently during childhood, humans would "play with toys" and be completely immersed in the activity. She imagined it looked something like what 9S was doing now.

Technically, she had come here before she went to the hangar. She hadn't talked to him because he looked so busy, but it had been three hours since then.

She needed to tell him to take a break. But all of a sudden 9S's shoulder tensed up, as if he were surprised from behind.

"Ah, it's just you, Operator."

9S relaxed his shoulder and looked over toward 21O.

"What do you mean, 'Ah'—I've told you that working so long without breaks is bad for you…"

"Yes. Yes!"

"Just one yes is fine."

"Yeah," he replied gloomily.

"Please disconnect from the terminal. I'm going to explain your next mission."

"What? I can't listen to you like this?"

"No. You need some exercise."

To think she would use the same line that 6O had used a few moments ago. But 9S needed more exercise than 6O.

"Let's walk a little."

9S somberly stepped away from the terminal.

"Where's the next mission gonna be?"

"The Abandoned Factory. Research of the facility and surrounding areas."

"Which means I'm alone again. That's so sad."

9S drooped his shoulders. But quickly raised his head and looked at 21O.

"Will you come with me, Operator?"

21O knew he wasn't being serious. He was definitely sad, but an operator accompanying him on a mission was out of the question.

"No. It's my job. Stop whining, and do the mission by yourself."

"I know!"

9S pouted. But he sounded a little dejected. *I guess I can be a little nice to him*, she thought.

"I hear the next mission includes field testing of new equipment."

"Really?" 9S asked eagerly. Just as expected, the word "new" got his attention.

"I'll give you the details in the hangar. I'll go over them as I get you acquainted with the new features."

"Yes!"

Suddenly, 9S flashed a look of concern.

"Is something wrong?"

Now that she thought about it, his behavior earlier had been a bit odd. She thought he was surprised by her entering the room, but 9S had looked in a different direction. 9S had reacted to something else.

"Something's…on my mind."

"What?"

9S surveyed the room, feeling like he was being watched. But 9S quickly shook his head.

"There's no way. It's probably just my imagination. Maybe I'm tired?"

"That's why I keep telling you to take frequent breaks…"

"Yes! Yesss!"

"One yes!"

She needed to force him to take a rest after she explained the details of the mission. Otherwise, his ability to perform tasks would suffer from the accumulated fatigue.

21O, thinking about such things, stepped out of the server mainte-nance room and urged 9S to do the same. He looked back into at the room one more time before he left, but again saw nobody there.

<That was cl0se.>
<He alm0st f0und us.>
<I wonder what "sad" means.>
<I d0n't kn0w e1ther.>
<Andr01ds are myster10us, aren't they.>
<Yeah. Myster10us and… fasc1nat1ng.>
<Let's play, a b1t m0re.>
<Yeah. Let's play… a b1t m0re.>

In the empty server room, the terminal displayed two words.

TRANSMISSION ENDED.

SMALL FLOWERS

by Yoko Taro

THE PARTICLES WERE SMALL, LIKE LITTLE GRAINS OF BLACK
SAND.

I found them inside of a human ruin.

I discovered an Android hiding inside of the structure, and exterminated it in a battle that lasted 5 days and 20 hours. I had reduced the enemy to rubble after slamming it against the wall. I found the particles as I was cleaning the remains.

There were several glass jars lined up on a crude shelf. Most of the jars were empty or broken, but one of them was still in good condition. I carefully lifted it, and saw inside a heap of tiny particles. Using the database, I was able to find that these particles were "seeds" of a "plant." But I couldn't find further information.

After staring at the jar for quite some while, I decided to take it back as research material.

■　■■

It's been several thousand years since the war began between the Androids and us Machines. Androids had impressive battle capabilities, and it wasn't rare for a hundred of us to fall before the attacks of a single Android. But we would win. By repeated self-regeneration and multiplication, we would simply outnumber them. A thousand of us if one hundred wasn't enough. Ten thousand if the thousand failed. We would repeat over and over, multiplying in the process. The most important resource in winning a war is time. Fight until we won. That was the greatest lesson in battle we had received from our creators.

However, we were completely indifferent to anything outside of battle. Since we were programmed by our creators to not use weapons of mass destruction in fear that they would destroy the environment, there were many species of living organisms that roamed the Earth. But we rarely went out of our way to research those organisms.

We gathered data about terrain and weather, solely because it would provide an advantage for battle. But living organisms were determined to be entirely unrelated to battle.

But was that really true?

It was a reach, but could these seeds contain the secret that would help rid us of the Androids forever?

I was going to see.

We had infinite time, after all.

So much time…

■ ■■

After consulting the network, it was determined that the individual that had discovered the seeds should carry out the research. In other words, me.

I looked through research materials from the past, but all I could find was that seeds were the infancy stage of plants. I couldn't find any information regarding how a seed transformed into a plant. So I had to start hacking the Android server.

The Android server had no considerable data either, but after a few days of searching through the human archives I found a file that instructed to "sow the seeds when the temperature is warm." Apparently it was a guideline to grow plants. But I didn't know how "warm" the temperature was supposed to be. Or where to "sow" the seeds. Why was the enemy so haphazard? They wouldn't be able to beat us like this…

For the time being, I selected a reasonable time to sow based on all of the climatic data we had gathered. I decided to sow the seeds in several media. To be honest, I wanted to exhaust all the possibilities at once, but I only had a limited number of seeds. I narrowed down the media to three: sand, concrete, and dirt. Records indicated that all these media contained living organisms at one point. But if my predictions were correct, dirt seemed to have the highest possibility to be correct.

Seven days later, I discovered the seeds had sprouted from the dirt. I reported to the internal network that my prediction had been correct.

■ ■■

Twenty-four days after I sowed the seeds, I ran into a problem.

The temperature had risen, and the plant had grown considerably. But several insects had attached themselves to the backs of the leaves. Upon further observation it seemed like they were stealing the plant's vitality.

The insects were small and I couldn't pick them off individually. Sprinkling water on them wouldn't shoo them away. I tried hitting them with a low-output laser, but it blew off the leaves of the sample as well. They were so irritating despite their small size—no, being small *made* them irritating. This concept was foreign to us Machines, as we strived to ever increase our mass and volume. Perhaps this was a good lesson. I chose to share it with the server as soon as I had all the data.

■ ■■

Eighty-five days since I sowed the seeds. Rain.

The insects had damaged the plant quite a bit. But the plant was still growing, and looked to have enough water to keep going. The intel I had gathered before had recommended that a weak to medium-strength alkaline water source be used, so I sprinkled some neutralizer in the water supply to maintain the alkalinity. But I wasn't sure if this method was the proper way to nurture a plant. Outside, there were giant plants that wrapped around buildings like snakes. How were those able to grow so big? Had they acquired a resistance to acid rain by adapting to their environment?

I looked down at the plant I grew.

I saw a flash of white between the leaves.

I carefully looked at the object.

It was a tiny, tiny part of the plant.

I searched through the data at hand.

According to Android data, that appendage was called a "bud," and it transformed into something called the "flower." There were dozens of pictures of flowers in the data. Red ones, pink ones, blue ones, white ones… there were innumerable types, but there weren't enough to determine what this plant would look like. That was okay. I would eventually find out.

I once again sprinkled some neutralizer.

This time, I only sprinkled just a little bit.

■　■■

One hundred and two days. Sunny.

The rainy season had passed, and the plant's flower blossomed.

The flowers in the data had been large, but the plant I grew developed a large number of small flowers, all about five millimeters in diameter. The type of plant was most likely usually different, but I could've made a blunder while growing it.

By the way, when looking at the plant recently, I felt an unexplainable feeling well up inside of me. I assumed that it was because the flower's shape reminds me of the moment gunpowder explodes.

Now that I thought about it, I hadn't had occasion to use my weaponry in a while. This was rare, especially as we Machines were made to fight. But growing this plant was an important mission. No matter how much I wanted to fight, I would never leave this plant and succumb to my desires.

The transmission suddenly came.

It was a short message, encoded 200 times over, and it took me, who was operating alone, four days to decode it. I knew what the affair was before even opening it. I've only received a few messages with such heavy encoding.

It was a strategic summary outlining the upcoming war with the Androids.

■ ■■

One hundred twenty-four days. Rain.

A part of my visual capabilities finally recovered on my twenty-fourth reboot. Scanning my body, I discovered that a third of my body was nonfunctional, and that half of my sensors were little more than scrap. I was lying on the ground.

The war took place eighteen days prior. I'd been prohibited from leaving my assigned area. Or rather, there probably wasn't enough time to give new orders to an experimental model like me. From the video footage I'd recorded, I had been ambushed by Android fire and rendered nonfunctional.

I tried to move my body, but I heard only a horrid grinding noise, and couldn't stand up. It seems I was considerably damaged. I was exasperated, since it would take about half a month for the self-recovery units I had on hand to repair me. With difficulty, I turned my head around to see a white blob. After focusing my camera, I realize it was the flowers I had grown.

Most of the plant had been blown away by shock waves and such, but a small part of it had been sheltered from any damage. Judging from how the parts around it were burnt to a crisp, it was almost a miracle.

A plant that doesn't move and myself, who couldn't move.

After recording the plant with my camera for a while, I initiated my self-recovery process.

My job was not over yet.

My mission was to see what would happen to this plant.

■ ■■

After that, the plant kept the flowers, unchanging.

I kept recording the flower. It had been twenty-two days since I rebooted, and I had completely recovered all my functions. During the battle I was cut off from the Machine network, which was a problem, but that didn't affect my horticultural mission.

I had learned what was needed to maximize a plant's growth potential from this experiment. What the right amount of water was, which temperature was appropriate, and what soil was optimal. Even in a downpour, or a storm, I dedicated myself to preserving the perfect environment for my plant.

The plant had recovered from the battle, and had developed even more flowers.

Now, when I looked at the flowers, I no longer felt anxious.

■ ■■

Two hundred eighty days since I sowed the seeds.

I discovered that a part of the plant had become brown.

I didn't think much of it since this had happened many times in the past, but this time the color spread day by day until it enveloped the whole plant.

I felt a response from one of my sensors. When I looked up, there was falling snow.

Detecting that the temperature had dropped, I placed a heater next to the plant and made sure to keep the temperature as close to constant as possible. I stayed that way for a few days, but the plant did not regain its typical green coloration. In fact, it looked like it was starting to fall apart.

For the first time in a while, I retrieved the reference data, and tried to find a method to fix the plant. But there was nothing useful in the data. All the entries recorded information up until the flower bloomed, or the fruit prospered, but there was no data about what happened after.

Several more days passed, and the temperature grew even colder. The frequency of days it snowed increased.

I decided to protect the plant by covering it with my hands.

I kept protecting the brown plant.

My mission was not over.

I needed to fix the plant.

I needed to understand and learn.

I will eventually fix this plant.

After all, I have all the time in the world.

A MUCH TOO SILENT SEA

by Jun Eishima

[7:30] Wake up ~ Breakfast

Her consciousness rose from the depths rapidly.

She could see something through her eyelids. It must be bright. She was irritated, and tried to pull her blanket over her head. "10H," she heard.

"Report: It's time to wake up."

"Sleepy."

"Recommendation: Wake up."

"No…"

"Warning: Wake up."

"Five more minutes."

Her body suddenly felt cold. Her blanket had been torn off her. Pod 006, the support unit of 10H, was as ruthless as ever.

"Ahhh. So annoying."

10H gave up and righted her body. She needed to stop resisting and just give in before 006 resorted to even more ruthless methods.

Pod used its four arms to deftly fold the blanket, and placed it on the edge of the bed. It put the pillow on top of that. It clarified how determined Pod was to not let her sleep again. 10H sighed as she looked along.

White sheets and a white blanket, along with a white pillow. The walls were white, the floor was white, and the ceiling was white. It was white all over. The only objects that had other colors in this room were herself and Pod—her black uniform and Pod's red body. No, perhaps one more: the room's display, depending on what it was displaying.

A voice from the monitor notified 10H that the water temperature and water pressure were at normal levels. This facility was buried deep in the sea, 10,000 meters below the surface of the ocean. Even slight changes in the environment could bring about disastrous results, which was why the surroundings were constantly being monitored.

"Report: It's breakfast."

Pod had already brought in a cart with her breakfast on it. *That's white too*, she thought. A white plate and a white cup. The cart that carried them was white as well.

"Recommendation: Eat it before it gets cold."

10H reached for the bread that was on the plate. It was square and flat, with some brown char marks on its surface. When she bit into it, her mouth felt dry. It was hard to swallow, so she washed it down with the liquid in the cup.

"Question: Is the toast crispy enough? Was the coffee a bit strong?"

"Not really…"

Pod could faithfully re-create human breakfast menus every day, but 10H never thought much of it.

"I mean, whatever. We can live without eating."

"Negative: Health comes from a healthy lifestyle. You must sleep well and eat well. Breakfast is an important source of vitality."

Vitality? What was that again? Ah, it was "The state of having energy sufficient to accomplish things." Pod often used ancient words from human civilization.

"It's such a chore. I have to excrete the energy surplus too."

It she didn't eat she wouldn't have to excrete. 10H thought it was a waste of time, but not according to Pod. "Good eating leads to good excretion," it said, which apparently gave way to a better mental state.

Of course, androids like herself could break down most foods. In other words, "excreting" was a rare last resort for them.

"Oh…"

The toast she was carrying to her mouth fell onto her plate. Looking closely, she realized that her fingers were injured. She had thought it was difficult to hold her cup because she was sleepy, but her hands were damaged.

"When did this happen?"

"Answer: That is the aftermath of moving goods."

"Is that…right?"

Yesterday some goods had arrived to resupply their stores. She did remember helping the Pods move them into storage, but had she worked that vigorously?

"Recommendation: Don't overwork yourself."

"Yeah, I'll keep that in mind."

Maybe her mental state was keeping her from remembering what had happened yesterday. Pod was right, she should probably eat proper meals.

[08:00] Scheduled patrol

It wasn't just 10H's room that was all white. This facility's walls, floors, and ceilings were all white as well.

It was hard enough to bring materials 1,000 meters underwater, so having an intricately decorated interior was out of the question. 10H had come here after the facility had already been made, so it wasn't like she knew this firsthand. It was only a hypothesis.

This facility, which was placed deep in the ocean where the water pressure was 1,001 hectopascals, was constructed there because it needed to be a secret from the Machines.

The emergency backup servers were located here. They contained data about the human board on the moon and every member of the YoRHa squadron. Human data was the most precious thing in the world.

"Server room 27, all clear."

Pod scolded 10H, who was eager to close the door.

"Warning: Check carefully."

"Well, I don't really understand anything that's going on."

Apparently there had to be sophisticated technology, and architectural modifications, to maintain a server this deep in the ocean. As a result, the whole operation was a jumble of components. A Type S might've figured it out, but a Type H, which specialized in healing and maintenance, had limited capacity to understand the environment.

And even if she didn't understand everything, Pod did. In server room 27 alone there were fifteen Pod 006s flying about.

Fifteen red Pods. Since the walls and ceiling were white, they stood out. It was a bit overwhelming. Their back-and-forth conversations filled the air.

"Suggestion: Since today is a bad day, can we reorganize the data another time?"

"Objection: We can't change the procedure at our convenience."

"Answer: I was just clarifying our options."

"Report: Anyway, today's lucky number is nine, apparently."

"Suggestion: Then should we work upside down?"

"Objection: No. Are you being serious?"

"Negative: Of course I'm joking."

What was this conversation? 10H's head hurt. It had no substance at all.

"Whatever."

Her thoughts were pretty meaningless too. There was nothing to do here, so she didn't have anything to think about. 10H's job was to maintain the Pods. If there was any damage or problems with the Pods, it was her job to immediately fix it. That's why a Type H was the resident assigned.

But the Pods hardly ever had any issues. And Pods would fix any slight issues themselves. Since first aid was part of their support role, they had simple recovery programs embedded in them. In other words, 10H had nothing to do.

She forgot how many months had passed since she was assigned here. She got a report every morning that noted how many days had passed and how many hours she had worked, but she had gotten tired of it and stopped listening.

"There's no red lights, so that means it's okay, right?"

"Roger: Yes, something like that."

"Okay, let's go to the next one."

She went out into the hallway, and climbed the stairs. Since the server rooms were interconnected like a web, this hallway had a lot of turns and slopes, as well as staircases.

"Ugh! Walking is so tiring!"

"Negative: Walking is exercise."

"I know that. But these shoes don't help…"

The soles of her shoes had magnets in them, which purposefully made it more difficult to walk. It did provide her with enough exercise just walking around the facility, but it made walking a burden.

"Recommendation: Don't complain, and just walk!"

"Ugh…"

"Recommendation: Where's your reply?"

"Yesss."

Once she climbed the stairs, she saw that the ON THE AIR sign was lit up. That was the broadcasting room. Apparently all the messages from the human board were gathered here before being broadcast to other locations. It was 10H's prediction that this was to keep the whereabouts of the human board a secret, but she wasn't sure.

She probably could have found out if she asked Pod, but she didn't particularly want to know. She had no interest in the subject of the broadcast either. She couldn't care less.

"Was today a broadcasting day?"

"Affirmative: There are 972 seconds left in the broadcast."

Today's my lucky day, she said in her head. She wasn't allowed in the room during broadcasts, so she could skip it. It wasn't good to skip the room in and of itself, but it just gave her a bit more free time.

[10:30] Free time

"I'm so bored…"

10H yawned as she moved a chess piece. After her morning rounds, there was nothing to do until lunchtime. And after she ate lunch, there was nothing to do until dinner. 10H's day was mostly free time.

"Recommendation: Cover your mouth when you yawn."

"What? Who cares."

"Objection: No. That's bad manners."

Pod 006 was being nettlesome. Other Pods were more perfunctory and talked less. Just like how 10H was the only android assigned here, Pod 006, the annoying and chatty Pod, was the only pod that was assigned here.

Usually Pods were manufactured in sets of three, but Pod 006 was a special model and a few hundred were manufactured. That's just how many of them were needed to take care of this facility.

Only one of them at a time orbited 10H. But since all the Pods looked identical, 10H wasn't sure if the Pod next to her now was the same Pod that had stayed with her yesterday.

Either way, since 006 only had one consciousness, it didn't make a difference. There were a few hundred units, but only one 006. That was hard for 10H to comprehend.

"Hey. Wait. Let me redo that!"

She had been carried away by her thinking, and failed to notice that she could've taken a piece.

"Objection: That's the third time. I told you I wouldn't let you after the last one."

"Only this time! It's only the third time today!"

"Objection: You said the same thing yesterday. How many times did I let you do that?"

"Uh…ten times?"

"Negative: Thirteen times. Don't act like you didn't know."

The number was too small to feign forgetfulness. Information of this scale would be preserved unless it was intentionally purged. This was the case for both 10H and 006.

"But my AI isn't specific to chess. A small correction shouldn't hurt…"

"Objection: No!"

Small sparks crackled from the end of Pod's arm.

"Okay, okay! No need for violence!"

"Roger: As long as you understand."

Pod used the now-sparkless arm to move the knight. 10H suppressed a smile with all her might.

"It's my turn, right?"

"Affirmative: Go ahead."

"This bishop is mine!"

"Suggestion: Wait! Let me redo that!"

"Nope!"

Just like 10H, 006 didn't have a chess-specific AI. Pods weren't made to think deeply to begin with, since it wasn't required for their mission tasks.

Even though they had good memory, what happened when an android and a Pod, who lacked chess-specific operations, played a game against each other? It became a silly matter of trying to distract their opponent with irrelevant talk, to lure them into making a mistake.

"I feel like at this point we're playing a different game."

10H pointed to the board with a chess piece. The bottom of the chess pieces used the same magnetic material that her shoe sole was made of, so a simple nudge wouldn't move the piece. The idea of having a metal board and magnetic pieces probably came from humans, so they could play in moving vehicles. Just like the coffee and toast, this facility was filled with references to human civilization.

"What's the point of two AIs playing a game they aren't specialized in?"

"Hypothesis: Because we're bored?"

"Well, that's true, but do we have to play a meaningless game to kill time?"

"Answer: An idle mind is the devil's workshop."

"What?"

"Answer: When you're bored you will occupy your mind with evil thoughts. That's why killing time is crucial. It's a proverb from ancient human texts."

10H was very skeptical that a human proverb would apply to her, but she didn't have any reason to deny killing time.

"Then, let's continue."

"Agreement: Then…"

"It's my turn!"

10H quickly moved her piece. Of course, she kept the bishop. A tiny spark flashed momentarily on the tip of Pod's arm. Perhaps it wanted to simulate clicking a tongue.

"But why are we so bored?"

"Answer: Being bored is a sign of peace. It's not a bad thing, is it?"

"I guess. That means the Machines haven't found out about this place."

If they were ambushed 10,000 feet underwater, it would be over. There was nowhere to run.

"Just in case, they should have assigned a Type B. No, since it'll probably be a defensive battle maybe a Type D?"

While this facility only stored backup data, it was important data nonetheless. Defending this was a tall order for a Type H.

"Negative: A Type B and Type D wouldn't be able to perform maintenance and repairs."

"Then maybe a Type S?"

"Negative: A Type S is easily bored. She wouldn't be able to deal with all the free time."

"Ah. I kind of understand now."

When it was needed, she would repair the Pods, and she never complained about the free time. In that respect, a Type H was most compatible with the role.

"But can you fight, Pod? I can't fight at all, you know?"

"Answer: I have a considerable amount of weaponry installed. I just don't use it regularly."

"I see. Then we're pretty safe."

There were hundreds of Pods, so they could just fight for her.

"Uhmm. Next is…"

She tried to move her rook, but it slipped from her fingers. The rook fell onto a pawn, and rolled onto the floor. She tried to pick it up, but couldn't.

"Hmm…my fingers aren't working very well."

They had been like this all morning. At first glance it was just a scratch, but perhaps there was deeper damage somewhere.

"I'm going to go repair myself."

"Objection: There are no spare digits in inventory. You'll have to wait until the next shipment."

"That's not for a while, right?"

She had helped with reshipment just yesterday after all. She didn't expect to injure herself while helping.

"I guess it can't be helped. I'll try recalibrating my program."

If she adjusted her grip strength and range of motion, she could probably at least reduce the amount of times she dropped things.

"I've had enough of chess today."

Leaving Pod to clean up the chessboard, 10H returned to her room.

[11:30] Investigation (Bedroom)

She dove into her own circuits, and inspected the program that controlled her fingers. She checked the defective areas and assigned the nerve-propagating algorithm to perform the calibration. *It's been a while since I've done Type H work*, she thought.

"I hope this'll do until the next shipment."

By recalibrating her fingers to keep ahold of chess pieces, her other functions would suffer.

For example, the strength she used to crush something between her fingers, and movements similar to that, would be compromised. If she wanted to crush a bug on a window, she would end up blasting a hole through the glass, and she would certainly destroy any touch panel or board she touched. The keyboard was in danger as well.

But she only needed to stay away from a touch panel until the next shipment, which wasn't too much of an inconvenience. She rarely used touch panels in the first place, and when she had to she could just make Pod do it. Fortunately, the facility had no machinery with keyboards, and had no bugs. In other words, this would hardly be a problem.

"Well, I'm bored anyway."

It was good that a slight defect wouldn't put her life in danger.

"Okay! Guess I'll finish. Hm?"

A strange thing in a strange place. Just like humans, androids didn't use their brains to their fullest extent at all times. There was always a part that was rarely used. It was necessary for emergencies, and it acted as a buffer in times of stress.

There was some odd encoded data in this usually empty part of her brain.

"What? Who did this?"

It would have taken a Type S or a Type H to do this. But 10H was the only android in the facility. Of course Pods were capable of doing this too, but they would have surely left a trace. Reading and writing onto a blank part of an android brain involved a difficult set of procedures. There was security in place so that only the individual could access it.

"I did this myself, right?"

She didn't remember at all. Had she used an operation that erased her memory after the task? And if so, why?

"Hmmm. Am I so bored that I actually forgot?"

She decided to decode the data. It was an encoding algorithm that needed the processing power of a Type S so she thought it would be particularly troublesome, but she ended up needing only two minutes to decode it.

"Ah. Yeah this was definitely me."

Knowing her own personality, she knew she wouldn't normally use such a difficult encoding. She was correct. The encoding algorithm wasn't simple, but seemed haphazard and almost rushed.

"But why?"

She wasn't sure. The encoded data contained coordinate data of the facility. And it pointed toward an area that was usually restricted.

"I don't understand…"

Turning her head to the side, 10H headed toward the location to which the coordinate data referred.

[11:50] Investigation (Hatch room)

The coordinate data pointed to the hatch room. The one room that connected the facility to the outside world. As a result, it was only used when they were restocking supplies.

The hatch was split into two sections, never open at the same time. There were many steps in place to stop ocean water from flooding the facility, given that it was constructed deep underwater.

"Such a chore…"

The first section was securely locked. Though she was rather incompetent, she was still the overseer of the facility, so she had permission to unlock the first section. If anything, the fact that she needed a password and black box authorization was more annoying.

Even though it was annoying, she didn't consider turning back. Something bothered her.

The door opened. At the same time, the whole first section was instantly illuminated. The walls, floor, and ceiling were pure white, and hurt her head.

"Question: What's wrong? Is there a problem?"

All of a sudden, Pod appeared. It seemed like it was worried, and was peering at 10H's face.

"It's okay. Nothing's wrong. I just have something I need to check."

She walked straight toward the door on the other side of the room. Section One was very large.

"Why is it so big? There's so much dead space."

"Answer: It's necessary to adjust the water pressure when there's water."

"I know that. I just think it's a waste to use it only for restocking."

10H put her hand on the door to Section Two. The encoded coordinate data was pointing up ahead.

"Objection: Don't. Access to Section Two is restricted."

She ignored Pod and opened the door. The lights came on, just like in Section One, and she saw a sea of white.

"There's nothing…?"

She thought there would be something here. A treasure chest, a bomb, or something that warranted leaving a message in the unused part of her brain. But there was nothing in the room. Nothing on the floor, the walls, or the ceiling.

"Warning: Danger ahead."

"Okay. I won't open the next door."

The other door in Section Two, which led outside, had a spindle-shaped door handle. If she opened it without adjusting the water pressure first, seawater would come rushing in with alarming force. She didn't want to imagine what would happen if water rushed in at 10,000 meters below sea level. At the very least, she and Pod would be crushed in an instant.

She walked to the location referenced by the coordinate data. Maybe whatever the coordinate data pointed to was not an object, but an event.

"Report: Withdraw immediately."

"I know."

Why this place? She slowly looked around as she walked. The floor and walls and ceiling were all white. The door from Section One to Section Two, and the door from Section Two to outside, were also white.

"Hm?"

She saw another color on the white door. There was a streak of black across the spindle-shaped door handle. It looked like something had been peeled off, or perhaps it was a scratch.

"I wonder what that is…"

She leaned in closer to get a better look. Suddenly, her vision was filled with stars. She felt a delayed pain to the back of her head. Pod 006 had hit her.

"What? Do you know your arm is freaking hard?" 10H complained as she turned around, and almost jumped out of her skin. She was looking down the barrel of a gun. Pod had transitioned to long-range attack mode.

"Wait! Stop!"

The first shot provided the answer. She thought she had barely dodged it, but she hadn't completely. An excruciating pain overwhelmed her upper arm. A red stain appeared on the floor.

She flung her shoes off. The magnets in the soles would only limit her ability to dodge. The second shot came. This time she was able to leap up. A laser struck the spot where 10H had been a moment ago. But it didn't leave a mark on the floor or the walls. She learned for the first time that this facility's walls and floors were heat-resistant.

There was nowhere to hide in the big room. She could only keep dodging. She kicked off of the floors and walls as she yelled.

"Hey! What are you doing? Explain yourself!"

Pod stayed in attack mode. It fired a third shot instead of giving an answer. She ran, but Pod predicted her escape route. Just as 10H dodged the laser, Pod struck her in the back with its limb. A moan escaped her.

She realized that Pod was seriously trying to kill her. Perhaps there was some kind of bug in its program.

She had to destroy Pod, some way or another. But how? Type H's were not built for combat. They realized their potential when they were with a Type B, which specialized in offense, and a Type D, which specialized in defense. Moreover, her enemy was a support unit. It was Type E's job to execute their comrades, not hers...

She didn't have time to think any further. The long-range lasers and short-range arm strikes flew at her relentlessly.

She felt a pain shoot through her side, and smelled burning flesh. She wouldn't be able to dodge the attacks completely much longer. But she had no weapon with which to retaliate. Regardless of whether she was fit to handle situations like this or not, she never carried weapons inside the facility.

Does that mean I have to fight with my bare hands? No way! I'm not a Type B, and my arm strength...arm strength?

What had she been doing just minutes before? She was calibrating her program so she wouldn't drop her chess pieces.

She quickly whipped around in a clockwise fashion. It hurt her damaged left leg, but she ran straight toward Pod.

Pod was in the middle of its firing sequence. 10H grabbed the barrel and twisted it up with her fingers. It crumpled softly beneath her fingers. She flicked Pod away with the fingers on her right hand. She curled her body to prepare for the impact. She heard an explosion above her.

It was a close call. She was able to bend the barrel because her fingers had been calibrated to a higher power output than normal. It was a victory by brute force. 10H sighed in relief, and felt a sharp pain. But she was so injured that she didn't know which specific injury hurt. She hadn't expected such an unfortunate event. What had happened—

But yet again her thoughts were interrupted. The emergency alarm alerting the whole facility to an enemy presence started to ring. *Why?* 10H thought. Why did the system think there was an intruder in section two? Pod and her were the only ones here.

She was confused, but she knew why in the back of her mind. 10H ran to lock the door separating Section Two from Section One.

The hundreds of Pods in this facility shared the same consciousness. They were different units from the one that had just attacked her, but their programming was identical. That meant that any Pod that came in here would attack 10H. The alarm wasn't a mistake.

She heard pounding from the other side of the now-locked door. The pods were probably throwing themselves against it. The jarring noise hurt her wounds. 10H grimaced and cowered in fear.

Now, there was no turning back inside the facility. The other door opened into the ocean. Ocean water 10,000 meters deep, at that. She had two choices. To be crushed by 1,001 hectopascals of pressure, or be burnt by the lasers from hundreds of Pods…

"I don't want either."

But it wasn't like she could stay still. She held her charred side, and started to walk toward the door leading into the ocean.

Pod was hiding something. And that something lay on the other side of this door. If she was going to die, she wanted to at least know what it was. She wanted to burn the image of it into her cornea before she died.

Although she might get crushed by water before that happened.

The moment she touched the spindle-shaped door handle, her fingers bounced off with a zap.

"Why?"

She looked back and forth between her fingers, which were burnt by an electric current, and the spindle-shaped door handle.

"That's weird. That's definitely weird."

Why was there a trap like this on the inside of the door? It would make sense if it was on the outside of the door, to deter enemies. But this made it seem like…

10H grabbed the handle again. Her hand burned. But she still spun the handle. The pain and heat made her vision go red. Her lips trembled. She didn't know what she was screaming.

The lever opened. She finally understood why the black mark was there. Someone had tried to open the door before, and kept on going as it burned their hand. The mark was the residue from that.

The lock was off. All she had to do was press a button to open the door. One push would...be the end of her.

She didn't have time to hesitate. The door to Section One was about to be compromised. 10H pressed the button. The door opened.

She didn't feel the sensation of being crushed. In fact, just the opposite. She felt a strong pull sucking her outside.

The sound of rushing wind only lasted for a second. Tranquility took its place immediately.

Her momentum sent her rolling on the ground. Grimacing in pain, she stood up. Rising sand obscured her vision.

"Sand? What? What's this?"

Her voice sounded strangely muffled. She must've damaged her vocal or auditory mechanisms when she fell. Her visual mechanisms seemed like they were defective as well.

Everywhere she looked, there was not a drop of water. Looking up, she saw a black sky, and the occasional stars that dotted it.

"No way..."

She couldn't believe her eyes. In front of her, in the black sky, was a floating blue sphere. It was Earth. Which meant that...

"Is this the moon?"

The moment she said those words it all made sense. There had been many tricks to make sure she never noticed the obviously weaker lunar gravity, which was a sixth of Earth's. YoRHa androids weighed about 150 kilograms, and ambulated thanks to extremely strong artificial muscles. Her control programs must have been rewritten.

The cups with lids, and magnets affixed to the soles of her shoes as well as the bottoms of the chess pieces— they were all to prevent 10H from realizing the difference between the gravity she expected and the gravity she experienced.

This wasn't 10,000 meters below sea level. The facility wasn't underwater at all. It was surrounded by sand and a soundless darkness.

What was I doing? What was I being forced to do?

She thought quicker than she had ever thought before. The pointlessly large hatch room, and complicated layout of the facility. The server room and broadcasting room. The ON THE AIR sign came to mind.

While that sign was lit, she was prohibited from entering the broadcasting room. Thinking back, that was strange. If it was just a broadcast, it wouldn't matter who was in the room. Yet 10H was prohibited.

This facility wasn't an intermediary station to keep the location of the original transmission a secret, this was actually where the transmissions were created. Everything fell into place.

Here, they didn't manage backup data, but instead the data of the human board. That was the secret that the Pods were keeping from her. And inside this white facility, there were only hundreds of Pods and her, so…

The human board doesn't exist. That means…humans don't exist anymore? Is that what it means? That is what it means.

Her legs gave out. 10H sat down right there. Sand rose silently around her. She was in danger of being crushed by a pain that wasn't coming from her wounds.

She felt the presence of Pods. Hundreds of Pods chased her.

Type B's were skilled at combat. If a Type D were to initiate a defensive battle, it would be problematic. A Type S would sniff out the truth. That was the reason. That's why she, a Type H, was selected to be the supervisor of this facility.

Even still, after a long time, 10H uncovered the truth. She was able to make it outside, sustaining damage to her hands in the process. She was quickly caught, and had her memory erased. That's why she had to resort to leaving a message in a normally unused part of her brain, which could only be accessed by herself.

The Pods surrounded 10H. This was it, but she wasn't scared. Her memories would be erased, and she would return to performing the same monotonous tasks every day. Her shock and sadness from realizing the extinction of humans would surely be erased without a trace.

"It's my loss. I give up. I won't give you any trouble."

She raised her hands. She let herself be restrained, and closed her eyes.

Just before her consciousness was sucked into darkness, 10H heard Pod's words.

"How unfortunate. This is the forty-sixth time."

MEMORY THORN

by Jun Eishima

THE CLOSE-COMBAT WEAPON FLASHED, SLICING THROUGH THE SANDSTORM. A Type-40 combat sword. A state-of-the-art weapon issued only to the elite forces on the front lines. The blade, crackling with electricity, burst and sent a semispherical object flying through the air in an arc.

A now-decapitated machine stopped moving. A few seconds later, its cylindrical body fell on its side in the sand and exploded, shrapnel showering two previously destroyed bodies in the vicinity.

After the explosion and shock wave, all that was left was the unique sound of the sirocco, the desert wind.

The dust eventually lifted, revealing a human silhouette. From the smooth outline of the shoulders, the tight waist, and the alluring legs that emerged from a short skirt, the silhouette clearly belonged to that of an adult woman.

All she could hear was the dry howl of wind. She couldn't hear any Machines, animals, or voices of humans. Well, to be precise, not the voices of humans, but of androids. In fact, she would never hear the voices of humans on Earth.

Humanity had pretty much left Earth. Due to the alien invasion, they had to flee to the moon. The Earth was at this point a war zone between the Machines, which were the minions of aliens, and the androids, who were sent to destroy them.

2B sheathed her sword as she called out behind her.

"Was that all?"

Responding to her question, Pod 042, which had been floating about ten feet in the air, lowered closer to the ground.

"Affirmative: No enemy responses detected within a five-kilometer radius."

"I see," 2B mumbled, as she approached the access point. Such points were disguised as human artifacts that were once called "vending machines," and provided transmission capabilities.

2B had come here to read some mail. But before that she had to go through the procedures, which was to destroy the Machines that gathered around the access point.

Even if the access point was disguised as a rusty artifact, Machines somehow knew that it was an important apparatus. Whether it be in the corner of a ruin or in the middle of a desert, the Machines gathered around it as if they were trying to prevent transmissions and intel collection. They didn't have a shred of intelligence, but they were crafty in strange ways. They were cunning to an annoying extent.

On top of that, no matter how many times they were destroyed, they just kept coming back. That tenacity was irritating. YoRHa squadron members were prohibited from having emotions, but she was still irritated. Especially when there was an important message to read, like today.

Either way, 2B could finally attend to her original errand. She opened her mail inbox on the display, and opened a newly received email. She had read the sender, the classification of top secret, and some of the message, when—

"2B!"

Suddenly appearing out of nowhere was Type S No. 9, aka 9S. While he was a YoRHa android, he wasn't modeled after an adult woman like 2B, but instead a teenage boy.

"Is that mail from Command?"

"No," 2B replied, trying to act casually.

"Anyway, why?"

"What? What are you talking about, 2B?"

"There should still be time before our mission begins."

2B had headed to the access point early because she'd received a mail notification from Pod. Even though it took her some time to clear the Machines, she had planned on reading through the message before 9S arrived.

"Well, I heard from the operator that 2B was in battle, so I thought I'd come in as support."

"No need to worry about me."

2B lightly shook her head, wanting to get rid of either irritation or panic.

"I guess."

9S dropped his shoulders with an exaggerated motion. Now she realized what feeling she wanted to get rid of. Their past conversations and experiences—she wanted to get rid of her memories of them.

"Well, since we were able to meet up, let's head toward the destination."

It was a déjà vu.

■　■■

"Ugh. More sand got in."

He couldn't learn to like the desert. It was the sand. If the wind blew it obstructed his vision and annoyed him, and if he walked it got in his shoes. It was kind of fun sliding down dunes, but otherwise the footing was poor and made it hard to walk. 9S scowled and looked at 2B, who was next to him. She was walking normally, without raising a brow.

"Doesn't it bother you, 2B?"

"What?"

"Aren't your shoes full of sand as well?"

"While it's uncomfortable, it doesn't disturb my walking, so…"

"Having sand in your shoes feels disgusting, doesn't it? It doesn't disturb my walking, but it's a matter of sanity."

"We are prohibited from having emotion."

"Roooger."

Although he agreed, he carried on the argument in his head. *2B should be the last person to say that*, he thought.

2B didn't control her emotions as well as she thought. At least, that's what 9S thought. Her catchphrase of "we are prohibited from having emotion" was probably more directed at herself than 9S. By saying that out loud, she was scolding herself. It was something the solemn 2B would do.

She doesn't have to try that hard, thought 9S. She could say it and still disagree with it at heart. Besides, how many YoRHa squadron members actually adhered to the rule?

But even if 9S said all of this, 2B wouldn't change her ways. 2B didn't have the dexterity to separate what she said and what she felt.

9S looked over at 2B's profile again. He saw a glimpse of something on her taut lips. 2B was also bad at hiding secrets.

"Nines?"

2B looked puzzled. She was probably caught off guard by his incessant staring.

"Uh. Nothing…just thinking since it's so dusty and hot it would be nice to take a bath."

That wasn't it. He wanted to say something else.

"We don't need to bathe."

"Right…"

What are you hiding? Recently you seem a bit down? Are you worried, or?

Even if he asked she probably wouldn't answer. He already knew that, after operating with her for a few months. Instead of his questions, 9S tried exclaiming, "Oh!"

"Could that be our mission subject this time?"

A giant shadow of what looked like a building loomed beyond the sandstorm. The end of the desert was near.

"Affirmative: That massive building is the main subject of this research mission."

Pod answered from the side. It was 9S's support unit, Pod 153. 2B's support unit, Pod 042, was silently floating behind her.

"Apparently it's called a temple. It's official name was "The Stone Temple," I think? People brought a statue of a god or something, and it started to be used as a temple."

There was a silence. 2B's mouth was stuck in a half-open position.

"2B? Is something wrong?"

Her mouth moved as if she wanted to say something, but 2B changed her mind and stopped. Her lips started to move again.

"No, it's nothing."

There was no way it was nothing. She'd hesitated too long. Of course, 2B had no intention of telling 9S why. Even though she'd started calling him Nines, it didn't feel like they'd gotten any closer.

"Let's get going, 2B."

9S intentionally used a bright tone, and started to run, as if he was excited to see the subject.

No matter how he asked, 2B probably wouldn't answer. He knew before he asked. That was unbearable for 9S.

■　■■

The stone temple was built in a deep chasm. Since there were cliffs surrounding it, it took a long time to get into the temple.

"They didn't have to build it so deep in the chasm—I don't understand."

After finally climbing down the cliffs and walking along the bottom of the chasm, they had to climb again to get to the temple's entrance—a treacherous path to get inside. It was hard not to complain.

"Hypothesis: The ruin surroundings were once a lake or a man-made moat, and humans used boats or a bridge to access it."

I see, 9S thought after hearing 153's response. Surrounding something with water was usually a technique that was used to protect someone or something important from outsiders. The temple was most likely built in the shape of a long cylinder to increase the floor area ratio.

"But I don't understand this…"

9S looked up at a giant tree. It seemed like it had died recently, and its black trunk leaned on the spiral staircase.

"Why would they plant such a big tree inside of their building?"

The cylindrical building had an atrium at its center, and the spiral staircase that started on the first floor cut off near the top floor. Perhaps before it had extended all the way to the top floor, but it was cut off now, and 9S couldn't tell what it had looked like in ancient times.

"What do you think, 2B?"

No response. She didn't realize 9S was talking to her. She finally realized 9S had turned around and was staring at her, at which point she asked a hurried, "What?"

"The spiral staircase."

He intentionally said something different.

"Um, I don't think much of it…"

She wasn't listening at all, just as he expected. If she had been listening, even just a little, she would have realized that he was talking about something else before.

"Let's go to the top floor."

Without mentioning that their conversation was broken, 9S turned toward the spiral staircase. 2B followed without a word. *This isn't like 2B,* he thought to himself.

Why was 2B acting like this even though she had a task to accomplish? Or was it *because* she had a task? 9S didn't say anything because 2B had been acting strange recently, and he had a hunch about why that was. He acted like nothing was wrong, and interacted with 2B the same way he had before. In contrast to 2B, who was bad at hiding secrets, it was a piece of cake for 9S. Otherwise, he wouldn't have tried to illegally access the server—and multiple times at that.

No, this wasn't about him. After all, he was about to be killed. He already knew. He even knew that 2B was tasked to carry out the deed.

He knew the moment this mission was assigned. That the research mission was just a front, and that 2B had a different responsibility.

Command ordered 9S's—or in this case my—*assassination. Isn't that right, 2B?*

But still, there was something wrong with how 2B was acting. She was too distracted. 2B wouldn't perform a top secret mission with this kind of halfhearted attitude. Even if Type S's were less suited for battle, they could counterattack and still assign Pod to assist in attacks.

Which meant that 2B was distracted not by 9S's unauthorized access to the server, but something else.

Suddenly, 2B, who was walking in front of him, swayed.

9S quickly extended both hands and caught 2B as she fell back.

"What happened? You never trip on stairs."

The spiral staircase was quite steep, and years of use and neglect had left various protrusions and holes. But with 2B's maneuverability, it shouldn't have been a problem.

"Are you okay?"

"Oh…yeah," she said in a distraught tone.

"There's fortunately no enemy signals, but if we were ambushed by Machines right now you would die."

"D-die…?"

9S didn't believe his eyes. 2B was smiling. Her lips were twisted unnaturally. This smile was strange, obviously abnormal.

"You've been acting weirdly. Are you feeling okay?"

"No…I'm…okay…"

2B's shoulders started shaking. Her muscles were going berserk.

"What are you saying? You're not okay at all!"

Why hadn't he seen this coming? No, he'd checked her before the mission and she was all clear. Since 9S handled maintenance for 2B; he would've requested a mission cancellation as soon as he saw a small defect.

"Let's call it a day."

But 2B ignored 9S, and kept heading toward the top floor.

"2B!" he said harshly as he grabbed her arm.

"Warning: Enemy signals above."

"Warning: Multiple signals at two o'clock."

The two Pods warned simultaneously. According to Command's research, the probability of running into Machines during this mission was supposed to be zero.

But heading from that direction were six flying types. They were what 9S would call "small fry," but they had signal-jamming capabilities. Which meant they couldn't be detected until they were in sight...

"This is terrible."

To think they would attack when 2B wasn't feeling well. Even if they chose to flee, they were in an atrium. They would just get attacked from above.

"Nines! Get back!"

He heard a sharp voice. 2B ran up the stairs with newly acquired vigor. She was moving more smoothly than before. She was back to the usual 2B.

"I'll support!"

Then he should support 2B, as usual.

"Pod! Analyze the enemies' flight patterns!"

He instructed 153, careful not to get in the way of 2B's Pod, 042. Each type of Machine had a unique movement pattern. If the androids could predict the movements, they could keep the damage sustained at a minimum while maximizing the damage they dealt.

Pod 153 shot down an enemy that was approaching 2B from behind. They didn't move that quickly.

9S saw light at the end of the tunnel, when the two Pods warned again.

"Warning: Enemy signal in the hallway of the top floor."

"Hypothesis: Multiple walking types. Specific types and number undetermined."

Because of the flying types' signal jamming, it was hard to tell what the situation was like. They needed to do something about that first.

"2B! Go! I'll handle the flying types!"

Type B's who specialized in close combat were more effective against walking types.

"Okay. I'll leave this to you."

2B jumped over the stair railing and ran. She grabbed onto 042's arm in midair, and glided into the hallway. There wasn't an ounce of hesitation in her actions.

"Pod! Take over the enemies by hacking!"

"Roger: Initiating support."

9S ran up the stairs and closed the distance between the flying types. Fortunately they were one of the types that were sluggish. It wasn't hard to infiltrate their cyberbrain dimensions.

Once he was inside, the Machines were powerless. They knew various ways to counter physical attacks, but hadn't adapted to handle internal attacks.

He found the control unit and wrote over the system. Even taking over one enemy would make things a lot easier.

He attacked the remaining five units with the one he took over. Perhaps they didn't have the resolve to attack an ally, as none of them retaliated. Even when 9S's unit attacked, they didn't evade and were obediently shot down.

After shooting down all five, 9S made the one he was controlling self-destruct, and left the digital dimensions. He raced up the stairs and headed to the hallway that 2B was in. He thought he would run in as support, but there was no need.

"It looks like you're done here."

There were a great number of metal fragments on the ground around 2B. They were the remains of walking types. There might be more on the top floor so they couldn't let their guard down, but it looked like the vicinity was clear of enemies.

"Are you hurt?"

"Not at all."

He felt relieved to hear that. All of a sudden, 2B's military sword dropped to the floor. 9S ran toward 2B. He had a bad feeling.

"2B!"

"It's okay. My hand just sl1pped, that's all…"

There was a strange noise mixed into 2B's voice. Her hands clawed at her throat.

"Logic virus?"

2B fell to her knees with a thud. 9S quickly tore off 2B's goggles. 2B's eyes were glowing red. There was no mistake. She was infected by the enemy.

"I'm going to eliminate it by hacking!"

"Wait…no…"

2B shook her head with great anguish.

"What are you saying? We need to get rid of it quick!"

It was a race against time. If infection of the personal data progressed, there was no saving her. 9S initiated hacking while 2B lay on the floor, still shaking her head.

■　■■

Various areas in the hacking dimension started to turn black. It was a typical logic virus infection.

The logic virus would take over the memory block and processing circuits, seizing control of the victim. Sometimes the victim would begin to indiscriminately attack their surroundings and comrades. *I'm okay if Command has me executed, but I don't want to die at the hands of a berserk 2B*, thought 9S.

"I need to hurry…"

Fortunately, he'd seen this type of virus. He'd succeeded in eliminating this one before.

"But it's progressed so far. And…"

An orange ball of light whizzed past 9S's personal data. It was an attack from the virus.

"This makes it tricky."

But the virus didn't look like it had evolved since last time, so its attack patterns were probably still the same. Which meant that he could carry on his task of eliminating the virus while dodging the attacks.

It didn't take too long for him to eliminate the virus. All that was left was for him to check for any other dormant viruses in the logic circuit. It was a simple task of running a high-speed search.

"Hm? That's weird."

He realized as he was searching that 2B's personal data was filled with blemishes. Usually the hacking dimension was perceived as a flawless white room. But this one looked rather shoddy, like one of the rooms in the ruins. He hadn't noticed until now because it had been covered in black because of the virus.

"Symptoms from the virus?"

He needed to go in deeper to investigate. Just then, he heard the sound of blowing wind and several words filled the space in front of him.

"We order you to assassinate 9S."

It was a fragment of 2B's memory. This was probably a line from an email. The sound of blowing wind was probably because she was in a desert. 9S pictured 2B receiving the email at the access point. This happened recently.

9S halted the search operation, and accessed the memory. His name had come up. Even if he wanted to forget that this ever happened, it was probably a good idea to see for himself.

"There were several attempts at unauthorized access into the main server. The other day traces of him were discovered in the memory blocks we use to keep top secret information."

The words were distorting. The sound of wind had disappeared. 2B had most likely been shocked in the moment.

"As such, we order you to assassinate 9S."

2B probably didn't want him to eliminate the virus because she was trying to hide this memory from him.

"You didn't have to worry about that. I knew already—that you were sent by Command as an assassin."

The only thing he didn't know was when she was going to kill him. That's why he had a suspicion the time had come when they met up at the access point in the desert. As he watched 2B read the message from behind, he sensed it was grave news. To top it off, 2B didn't notice him approaching from behind until he called out to her.

"Head destroyed."

He was caught off guard. There was a random memory fragment stuck inside this one of 2B reading the message. It was a low voice with no inflection. But it sounded so much like 2B's, he had to clarify.

"This is 2B. The task has been completed."

It was the same voice. If those were 2B's words, whose head had she destroyed?

He moved toward a mess of memory fragments.

"What's this?"

The memories looked disheveled at first glance, but upon further inspection they twisted and entwined in an unnatural way. Every fragment had thorns sticking out of it. He had never seen memory data that looked like this.

Thorny, twisted, and entwined—memories of 2B.

Maybe he shouldn't look. Maybe he shouldn't know. But he couldn't stop himself. He was a little spiteful toward the tremendous curiosity that Type S's had.

The moment he touched a fragment, an immense pain cut through him. That pain ironically cleared 9S of any doubt. He had to go on.

"But a Type S could never beat a Type B."

This voice. This was 9S's own voice. This was from 2B's memory, so he must have said this in 2B's presence. But he couldn't remember at all. It seemed his memory had been erased.

Who? Why?

9S accessed another memory to find the answers.

"Bye, 2B."

This was his own voice too. 2B was desperately trying to keep calm as she heard his faint voice. There probably wasn't any visual data because 2B had shut her eyes.

"Bye, 2B."

"Bye, 2B."

"Bye, 2B."

The same words over and over. Apparently these words had been going through 2B's head ever since she received the message from the commander in the desert.

When and where had he said these words?

The memory switched. He could see scenes from their mission at the Sand Temple. This was a memory from the first time 2B killed 9S. It was a plan to trap 9S in her own cyberbrain dimension and destroy him after trapping him in with a self-shutdown algorithm.

The words were what 9S had said to 2B right before he was deleted in the cyberbrain dimension.

"2B had killed me before."

He understood. This was the reason why 2B seemed so distracted.

He accessed the other fragments. He felt more pain, but had no intention of stopping.

This execution happened in space. 2B destroyed 9S while they were heading to Earth. The next happened once again in the Sand Temple. Perhaps she had learned from the last execution, because this time 2B slashed 9S as soon as they stepped into the temple. There were a few times in the Stone Temple as well.

There were times when 9S was killed after they had gone on a few missions together, and times when he was killed before he really knew who 2B was.

No matter how many times he was killed and his memory was erased, 9S always eventually reached the conclusion that Command was hiding something. And he would stop at nothing to uncover the truth, even if that meant trying to access the main server without authorization.

2B tried to stop him many times. If she operated with 9S, she did her best to convince him that there was nothing suspicious about Command. When she killed him without getting to know him, she always erased more of his memory than necessary to make sure it was rid of any inklings of doubt.

But all of 2B's efforts were in vain. No matter how hard she tried the result was always the same. If she was warm or cold to 9S, if she called him Nines or didn't, the assassination order always came.

"So that's what happened…"

It had bothered him ever since he met 2B. There were times when they were alone, but it seemed like 2B was talking with another Type S. At the time, he concluded that she must've worked with Type S's in the past.

His hypothesis was correct, in a way. She had been working with 9S the whole time. Just different versions of him.

"If we were ambushed by Machines right now you would die."

He understood why 2B had started acting strangely after he said that. 9S had said the exact same line in the exact same situation before, and 2B had killed him right after that. Hearing him say that hurt 2B.

It wasn't just this one either. All of 2B's memories of him hurt her. So much that her personal data had started to deteriorate.

"I won't apologize. It was a mission. She had no guilt. Never."

9S looked around at 2B's personal data once again. It was white, but full of scratches and on the verge of falling apart…

■ ■■

She awakened from the darkness. After one blink, she saw 9S's face in front of her. But was it just her imagination? He had a sort of dark expression. 2B blinked once more, and stared back at 9S.

"Nines…?

That's right, she was ambushed by Machines, fought them, and was infected by a logic virus. The last memory she had was of her trying to adamantly refuse 9S's hacking.

"I eliminated the virus."

She wasn't able to stop him. 9S had forcefully hacked her, and entered her memory block.

"So…you saw everything?"

9S gave a silent nod.

"I see…"

She wasn't surprised. She knew this day would come. Type S's were sharp. He had even seen through her top secret missions a few times in the past.

"So 2B wasn't your real name, was it?"

Well, this is a new turn of events, she thought.

"2E."

It was the first time 9S had called her by her real name. Type E No. 2. Her YoRHa model specialized in executing deserters and traitors, or putting an end to wounded comrades on the battlefield—that kind of dirty work.

2B drew her sword. 9S's shoulders twitched. This 9S knew that she'd killed him many times in the past.

"I have no intention of killing you anymore."

She pointed her sword at herself, and pushed the hilt into 9S's hands. "Kill me."

The mission had failed. She was disqualified as a Type E. She was a defective product unworthy of even her operational costs.

"At least at your hands…"

There was no way this would completely make up for her past actions, but if it even atoned for one ten-thousandth of the pain she had caused 9S, that's what she wanted. This was the only thing she could do.

She saw 9S grip the hilt. 2B smiled and waited for her death.

The sword flashed. But it didn't head toward 2B.

"Nines?"

2B's eyes widened as she was showered by red liquid. 9S slowly fell after tearing his own throat open. She held him. "Why?" Her voice sounded distant.

"Because it was…fun."

She couldn't believe her ears. It was fun? Impossible. There was no way.

"It was fun to be with you. My past selves probably would have said so too."

"Nines…"

She tried to say sorry, but 9S interrupted her.

"Don't apologize. Instead…"

9S heaved, as a smile flashed across his face.

"Next time…don't hesitate, and just kill me. We'll see each other… again."

She could meet 9S again if she deleted his entire memory block and reinstalled his personal data. Even if it wasn't the current 9S.

"Because…I…want to…see you…again…"

Even if their next meeting was for an execution.

"Okay."

She couldn't tell what kind of face 9S made, because her vision was blurry.

His body became limp. The sword dropped from his hand, which had been on 2B's cheek. His black-box signal weakened further and further. It would be vile to let this last any longer.

9S laid his body down, and stuck the sword through his chest. The black-box signal completely diminished.

"I promise."

She was going to kill him, without hesitation. The next time, and the one after that. Not because it was her mission, but because it was 9S's wish. To honor his wish of seeing each other again—she would kill him.

2B quietly slid the sword out of 9S's chest.

RECOLLECTIONS OF EMIL

by Jun Eishima

I MOVE THROUGH THE DIM FACTORY, KEEPING MY FOOTSTEPS AS QUIET AS POSSIBLE. Well, they aren't footsteps. Right now I am nothing but a head. The other day I was trying to get home when I fell off a ledge and destroyed my body.

My head is harder than a rock but my body breaks really easily. It would be nice if I could make a body that was as strong as my head, but that's probably impossible.

Besides, a body has to be not only strong but practical. I've made a "self-defense force armored vehicle" before, but for its size it didn't carry much luggage.

I've tried using a "pickup truck" that specialized in mobility, but it broke down in a day. If it broke from falling off a cliff, it wouldn't hold up when I do business in the city ruins.

Oh, I run a shop. A portable shop. I started it because…um…I'm pretty sure there was a good reason. I forgot, it was a long time ago.

Anyway, I really need to remake my body, so I infiltrated this factory. I can get a lot of materials here.

I'm thinking of using a three-wheeled body instead of a four-wheeled one this time. I fortunately found some remains of a three-wheeled truck. The body was rusted and the tires were flat, but with some magic it'll be no problem!

According to some ancient documents this truck was a best seller in areas with muddy or bumpy roads. There's some video data, so I'll be able to perfectly re-create it!

Now, on to the materials. First, natural rubber. I need to do something about those tires.

But this area is full of dangerous Machines. It used to be called "Robot Mountain," so maybe they feel comfortable here. I need to make sure I don't run into them.

Hm? I can smell some natural rubber! Is it this way? Yep, it is. This is the smell of high-quality material!

Excited, I move toward the direction of the smell.

"Wowowow!"

I suddenly have steam billowing over me, and I can't see anything.

"Hm? I'm moving?"

I feel my head being carried away. Is this what they call a conveyor belt?

"Woah! What's this?!"

There's a line of robot parts. They're being carried away somewhere in one straight line.

"I need to run...wait, what?!"

An arm extends from above and grabs my head. Two half-spheres approach me from the sides.

"Stop!"

Clop it goes as I am enveloped in darkness.

"No! Let me out!"

No matter how much I yell or struggle, I am trapped in darkness. And exhausted from screaming so much, I fall unconscious...

"Huh? Where's this?"

It is suddenly bright, and standing in front of me are a woman and boy I've never seen. "What is this..." they say, as they tilt their heads. But my head is tilted too!

"Ummm. Who are you?"

I know they are androids, but...

"It looks suspicious. Let's destroy it, 2B."

What?!

"Wow no! Wait!"

I'm not suspicious! If anything you two are the suspicious ones! You're wearing all black! And wearing black blindfolds!

"I'm going to destroy it."

"Ahh! Stop!"

I escape at my top speed. I think I bumped into something, or broke something, but I didn't have time to check.

…Did I lose them?

I slow down and look back. Then feel something weird.

"Boing?" Was that the word for it?

It seems I bumped into something and was bounced back.

"Hm? Feels furry?"

I felt warm wind from above…

"Uh, um…"

Looking up, I see two tusks. What I thought was wind was the breath…of a boar. Which meant I bumped into the side of a boar. I slowed down right before, so it wasn't a life-threatening impact, but it must've hurt him to be hit by my rock-hard head.

Which means that…you must be really mad right?

"I'm so sorry!"

Oh no! It's running after me! I hate boars! I'm always being chased by them! When they hit me it hurts!

"Don't come near meeee!"

It's hard to run away right now! There's tons of leaves in my face! I hear branches snapping right beneath me! But the boar is still coming after me!

Ah!! I'm going to hit it I'm going to hit it! I'm going to crash into that big tree!

I just managed to swerve out of the way. I must've lost the boar… wait, it's still coming after me! It seems like this boar has drifting capa-bilities. There's always a few of them. The high-functioning boars.

Why am I thinking of something like this—hm? Where's the ground?

"Aaaah!"

It seems I rolled off a hill. It hurts. It feels like I'm dying. It feels like I'm getting beaten with sticks. Well, I'm actually just bouncing off boulders here and there.

I wonder how long I rolled about. Before I knew it I was at the bottom of a dim valley, feeling dizzy.

Sigh. That was terrible. Well, at least I lost the boar.

"Hm? I smell some iron here?"

Iron ore is an essential material to make a body as strong as my head!

After being chased by a boar, I thought I was unlucky to roll all the way down into a valley. But I think I'll be able to turn misfortune into fortune. Let's go pick some iron ore!

Yes, yes it's here! There's some high-quality iron ore! I can take as much as I want! This is fun!

"Heave-ho! Pick this up pick this up and pick this up! Pick that up and pick this up! Phew!"

As I am singing playfully like so, I suddenly hear the sound of grinding metal behind me. As if some Machine is walking around…

"It wasn't my imagination!"

There's Machines! And lots of them! I thought I'd turned misfortune into fortune, but I was unlucky after all…

I use magic to absorb iron ore as I roll around, and manage to narrowly escape the valley. I go home and visit the factory ruins again to get natural rubber. I finally have all the materials.

Time to go to work. First I use the natural rubber to re-create the tires. Three spanking-new tires. Reliable tires that can travel over rubble without a problem!

Next I have to clean the rusty truck. I line up all the iron ore I collected and…

"Emil Beaaaaaaaaaam!"

The iron ore is turning into a puddle. According to the data, the ideal temperature for manufacturing iron is 2,000 degrees Celsius. This way, you can separate the impurities and pig iron. Of course, I won't throw away the impurities. They can be divided and cooled for later use. I'll need them for something…probably.

Okay! Now this part is a race against time. Strike while the iron is hot! That's what some ancient texts said.

"Yeahhhh!"

It's done! I coated the truck in iron, and now it looks brand-new!

Now we just have to attach the tires, and we're done.

Then I screw my head on the body so it won't roll off. There's better ventilation when I use screws instead of gluing myself on.

I make sure to display my products on the truck bed instead of just throwing them on. This advice was in the texts too. "Pay attention to the layout of your booth to increase sales!" it said. Another tip was to "Make sure customers can see it from far away!"

So I decorate the truck bed, and put up a shop flag, and add a loud-speaker. I hope I get a lot of customers…

Oh right, this time I did a full model change, so I have to record my thoughts on its durability and usability.

So starting tomorrow, Emil's shop will be open!

[Day One]

My new body is working really well. It rides smoothly on rocky hills and grassy plains! I understand why it was a top seller in areas with bumpy roads.

But I noticed the texts were right when they explained that a three-wheeled car topples easily navigating sharp turns. There's a certain nuance to balancing this body. I have to be careful.

The amplifier cracks a little bit, so maybe it needs some adjustment. I hope the volume doesn't bother anyone.

I hope customers come. I'll work hard tomorrow too.

[Day Two]

The new body is great, but my sales aren't. I need customers. I'll work even harder tomorrow!

[Day Three]

Today the weather is really nice. I'm in a good mood, so I'm hopping around from one building to another.

"Recommendation: Force interruption with long-range attack from Pod."

I hear somebody's voice, I think. I hear a gunshot, and start to spin around as my gears shudder…my engine stalls. So that's what they meant by a forced interruption…

"Ow ow ow."

I slowly get up as I hear footsteps heading toward me. I look up, and am surprised.

"Oh, it's you, from the other day!"

The Androids in black. The other day they had decided to destroy me right away, so I guess they're more violent than other Androids. I remember it now. This is just like…just like…wait? Who does that remind me of?

Oh well. Business, business. They're my customers too.

"My name is Emil. As you can see, I run a shop. Would you like to purchase anything today?"

Since my reopening, they're my first customers. I hope they buy a lot of stuff!

"Would you like a rusty clump? And I would recommend a rusty clump? Also just so you know, the rusty clump is a good deal!"

Apparently the woman in black is named Ms. 2B and the boy in black is named Mr. 9S. The two buy the titanium alloy. Even though I recommended the rusty clump…

"Thank you very much! I'm looking forward to your next visit!"

I hope they start coming regularly. Oh, I have business to do!

"What? Where do I live?"

"We didn't ask."

This is business. Answering a question they didn't ask, that's what a good salesman does!

"Um, I live deep underground…deeper than the deepest part. Come play with me anytime."

After watching Ms. 2B and Mr. 9S walk off, I decide to call it a day. I need to tidy up my home if they are going to come visit.

[Day Four]

Today I've been doing repairs since morning. Yesterday the "long-range Pod attack" knocked me off my wheels and gave my body a small dent.

Well, it's not too bad. I'll be able to finish repairs before breakfast. Well, I already ate breakfast, but…

Anyway, first I have to inspect the damaged part. Hmmm…it looks like the sides need to be more durable. After all, in the city ruins where there's tons of rubble, tumbling around is a normal occurrence. I should probably use some spare material to reinforce the sides.

Time to work. I lined up the iron ore and…

"Emil Beaaaaaaaaaam!"

Take out the impurities, and…ah! I'll try adding some titanium alloy. And some memory alloy too.

"Emil Cyclone!"

The iron ore, titanium alloy, and memory alloy start mixing together. Now I have to coat this with magic.

"Yeah!"

Okay. All right. It looks good. Repairs and reinforcement are complete. Now, maybe I'll eat.

"Hm? Huh? Did I already…eat breakfast? It seems I did, but maybe I didn't. Which one was it again?"

I can't remember. Every time I repair my body I lose some memories.

"Oh well."

I'll eat breakfast.

[Day Five]

Today I'm restocking my shop. Yesterday I cleaned up a weapon I found, and it turned out better than expected! It's a masterpiece!

I need to go sell it right away. Someone will be happy to have it!

I quickly leave my home. I blow by familiar-looking areas in the city ruins. I'm gunning it, at high speed, because I want somebody to buy it as soon as possible.

Am I going too fast? I hear a gunshot, and start to spin around as my gears shudder—yes, it's Ms. 2B and Mr. 9S.

Ms. 2B is relatively quiet, but it seems like Mr. 9S talks a lot. He seems really curious too, and always has a look of fascination as he talks.

"Hm? Why do I run my business in this form? Well I could talk about that for days..."

I think we should talk about that when you come over for some tea. It really is a long story. Because a long long time ago...a long...hm? What was it again?

No, now's not the time to think about that. It's all about business.

"Anyway, won't you buy something today? I have some incredible weapons in stock today. Like Angel's Folly and Type-3 Fists. Angel's Folly and Type-3 Fists."

I repeat myself because they were my top recommendations. As a result, Ms. 2B and Mr. 9S bought both of them. They looked happy. I'm glad, I'm glad.

After I come home it's time to inspect my body. Since I reinforced the sides, I don't see any dents today. Although there are a few scratches.

On the other hand, my brakes are starting to wear out. Speeding doesn't seem like the best idea.

[Day Six]

I went off my usual route and tried business around the steel tower. Doing the same thing every day just leads to fatigue. It's important to try new things.

There's a lot of weeds growing near the steel tower, so it's a bit hard to ride around. But only an amateur salesman would be discouraged by that! A true professional goes to the customer, wherever they are! It's my duty to transport goods!

That's right, because I'm...um. Hm? What was it again? I was about to remember something...

"Oh! That's!"

Somebody's crossing the bridge over the valley. Those black clothes definitely belong to Ms. 2B and Mr. 9S. They cross the bridge and head toward the shopping center. That's where I'd met Ms. 2B and Mr. 9S for the first time. What a glorious moment. Even though it was a little scary.

Hmm, maybe I'll ask them how they like the weapons they bought last time. I wonder if they're useful. I wonder if Ms. 2B and Mr. 9S would be happy to hear I'll do maintenance for them.

And so I decide to cross the bridge and follow the two of them...but the bridge is creaking a lot. Is it going to fall under my weight?

Oh, I just have to use some magic! This is the perfect time for magic! I don't know if I can fly very well in this form, but...

"Whoo!"

I'm able to float. I only get off a couple feet off the ground because my body is so heavy. But this is good enough for crossing the bridge.

I quickly head to the other side. The entrance to the shopping center is littered with boulders and rubble, so I just float over them.

"What a strange flower."

I can hear Mr. 9S. The floating box next to him—I think it's called a Pod, right?—say, "Answer: It's a type of plant known as a lunar tear"

I widen my eyes when I hear what the Pod said. Lunar tear? I feel like I've heard the name "lunar tear." Looking closely I can see a white flower near Mr. 9S and Ms. 2B's feet. It looks familiar.

"Lunar tear…"

"Ah! Since when have you been here?!"

Mr. 9S looked back in surprise.

"This flower is called a lunar tear, right?"

Where? Where have I seen this flower before? I really want to remember, but I can't…

"Looking at this flower brings back a lot of memories. I don't know why, but I remember being chased by a huge boar a bunch of times…"

That's probably why I'm so afraid of boars. But I feel like there was always someone next to me when I was being chased by boars. I try my hardest to remember who that person was. Was it just my imagination?

"My body was always broken, and I had to try different replacement parts…"

"That sounds pretty intense."

My body wasn't nearly as strong as my head. Even now, I'm testing a new body after my model change.

But I feel like back then I was making a different type of body. That's weird…what I need is a body that specializes in transporting goods.

"And…when I look at this flower I'm filled with this weird feeling. My chest feels tight."

What is this feeling? It's sad and lonely. But then again it's warm and painful. As if someone mixed all the metals into one alloy but it somehow ended up becoming an entirely new metal.

"Um. I want to ask you a favor, is that okay?"

It might be rude to ask a customer for a favor. But I can't help myself. I need to find out.

"Please let me know if you ever find lunar tears growing in other places. I want to find out why I'm feeling this way."

Where is this feeling coming from? What is this feeling for?

"So please. If you find any lunar tears, please send a transmission to this frequency."

"Okay."

Ms. 2B's answer was short, but kind, and so similar to someone…

[Day Twelve]

Mr. 9S's transmission comes in as I am riding around a building that had started leaning.

"Yes, what is it?" I answer a bit nervously. It is definitely about the lunar tears.

"I found a lunar tear. The location is…"

The location data is pointing toward the desert. I'm at the entrance of the desert right now. How lucky!

"I'm coming right away! Please stay right there!"

I need to go as quickly as possible! The faster the better! Faster, faster! …Yeah!

"Sorry to make you wait!"

"Wow?!" Mr. 9S yelled. There is no reason to be that surprised. Anyway, about the lunar tear. I look down near Ms. 2B's and Mr. 9S's feet.

There is a white flower growing from the sand, waving in the wind. These colors—sand and white petals. I've seen this. These colors.

"That's right, this place…"

"Did you remember something?"

"A long time ago, I remember taking care of this flower."

It took a lot of care to grow this flower. It needed to be in the right temperature, humidity, and had to be watered at specific times…

"But the sand slowly ate away the plant, and the flower started to die…"

I didn't want it to die. I wasn't allowed to let it die. But the sand and dry air had no mercy.

"That's right, I stopped seeing humans around that time."

"Humans?"

Wolves filled the desert and humans disappeared from the surrounding cities…I was all alone. Hm? That's weird. I feel like I wasn't alone yet? But why? My memories are getting all mixed up.

"Thank you for finding it. If you find any more, please tell me."

I might remember more if I see other lunar tears in other places. My memories are probably all over the place because there's some missing parts.

"I'm…going to stay here for a bit…"

I'll keep watching this flower a little longer.

[Day Sixteen]

The next time Mr. 9S contacts me, my tires are stuck in some rubble and I am stranded.

"Yes, what is it?"

But I kind of know what Mr. 9S is going to say. Probably something along the lines of, "I found a lunar tear…"

"I found a lunar tear. The location is…"

Just as I thought. I was right.

"I'll go right away! Please stay there!"

I can't stay stranded. The path from here, the crater zone, to the amusement park is pretty complicated.

I need to hurry. I need to get there quickly. The faster the better! Faster, faster!

…Yeah!

"Sorry to make you wait!"

"You always get here so fast!"

Mr. 9S is really shocked. There's really no reason to be that surprised.

Anyway, the lunar tear. I look down near Ms. 2B's and Mr. 9S's feet.

Right below an emergency exit sign, almost hidden by rubble, is a white flower.

The sound of fireworks, interrupting the music played by the robots. Low, but erratic and sharp sounds.

"That's right. This place is…"

The sound of gunfire. Heat and the smell of something burning.

"A long time ago, aliens invaded Earth. I fought desperately to protect Earth, right in this very spot."

I need to vanquish the aliens. I need to drive them away from Earth.

That is the new fragment of a memory I recalled. A memory of a battle so stressful it made me anxious just thinking about it.

"You did, Emil?"

"Yes. I probably had something I needed to protect. But I don't remember what that something was…"

There's no memory of that something in my vague recollection. I know it was important and something I didn't want to forget, but I don't remember.

"Thank you for finding it. If you find any more, please tell me. I'm going to stay here for a bit."

I want to keep watching this flower…but the more I watch it, the more pain I feel. That's what I feel.

[Day Nineteen]

I am searching for materials in the Abandoned Factory when Mr. 9S sends me the third transmission.

"Yes, what is it?"

This is probably about a lunar tear as well. I need to check Mr. 9S's location data.

"I found a lunar tear…"

"I'll come right away!"

It is quite a way to the Flooded City, where Mr. 9S was. I panic.

I need to hurry. I need to get there quickly. Faster, faster, the faster the better!

…Yeah!

"Sorry to make you wait!"

"As always…you're fast."

Mr. 9S seems more amazed than surprised. Anyway, the lunar tear! I look behind Ms. 2B and Mr. 9S.

There is a white flower growing from a crack in a boulder. It looks like it is holding on for dear life in the sea breeze. The sound of waves is harsh.

"Ah, that's right."

This beach. The flooded city, and the sound of seagulls.

"What happened here?"

"The battle against the aliens," I replied. It happened here. I was responsible for this area around the beach.

"The battle conditions only got worse with each passing day. I cloned myself so I could win in battle."

Since the enemy fought with numbers, we needed to fight with numbers too.

"But the number of enemies kept growing. And I lost many of my friends."

I had no time to mourn the death of my friends. I kept cloning myself, and increasing the number of casualties. It was just a repetition of that cycle.

"This happened a long time ago."

"I see," replies 9S. He suddenly looks up.

"Emil, how long have you been alive?"

"I don't really know."

I feel like I've been alive so long I forgot, but I also feel like I've only been alive for a short time. I don't know anything for sure.

"I didn't need to know to fight."

We only had to worry about how to get rid of the aliens. That was all.

"Thank you for finding it. If you find any more, please tell me. I'm going to stay here a bit."

I want to keep watching this flower forever. But I also want to stop remembering. I'm scared to remember more.

[Day Twenty-Three]

I am already checking Mr. 9S's location data when he contacts me. I already know I have to be there.

…Yeah!

"Sorry to make you wait!"

"I haven't even contacted you yet…"

The moment Ms. 2B and Mr. 9S appear right in front of me, I realize I have been using teleportation this whole time. That's how important the lunar tears are. Flowers so important I would do anything to see them.

So I have been using magic this whole time. Powerful magic, but I hadn't noticed one bit.

That's right. This powerful magic originally belonged to…and this flower was…

"Emil? Are you okay?"

Mr. 9S's worried voice snaps me back to reality.

"I remembered right now. I'm…"

"Huh?"

"No, thank you very much. Because of you I was able to remember something very important to me."

"Something important?"

"Yes. A place that was very important to him."

He had treasured these white flowers and his memories associated with them. I had forgotten all about him.

"To show my gratitude, I'll take you to that place."

I take out an old key. I forgot about this too, but I didn't lose it. I kept it with me even though I didn't know what it opened.

"This is a key to an elevator in the shopping center."

Maybe it wasn't a coincidence that I met Ms. 2B and Mr. 9S there, or that they had found a lunar tear there.

"I'm sorry, please go on without me. I want to stay here a bit longer."

I am still in shock. I remembered so many things at once that I am confused. I need time to calm down and organize my thoughts.

It doesn't take too long for me to organize my thoughts. Maybe I had already prepared myself for when I remembered, so I'd be able to do what I have to do.

The shopping center elevator runs just like it used to. The sound the compressor makes when the doors close and open, the erratic shaking, everything is the same.

Right as the doors open on the bottom floor, I hear Mr. 9S's voice. Apparently the two of them had just arrived as well.

"Wow! There's so many lunar tears!"

"What is this place?"

The two look around in shock. They probably hadn't imagined a sea of white flowers blooming deep underneath the shopping mall.

"Thank you for coming here."

Ms. 2B looks puzzled and says, "Emil, what is this place?"

"This was the place I wanted to protect. Well, to be more precise, the place the person I used to be wanted to protect."

Mr. 9S tilted his head. "I don't understand."

They want to know more, so I start to talk. A story I thought I would never tell, the story of "us."

"A long time ago, I was originally constructed as a weapon."

"A weapon…"

Long before the aliens invaded Earth. Back when there were lots of humans. I, the person I was, was just a normal human child. Until I was modified into an experimental weapon.

"When the war against the aliens began, I cloned myself to increase our numbers."

"Cloned yourself?"

"Yes, I'm one of the many Emils that were created at the time."

That's why the one that cloned himself was not me, but the person I used to be—the original Emil. He wanted to protect the Earth, no matter the sacrifice. He felt that way because it was where his friends, who were more important to him than his own self, lived.

"After cloning, I, or rather we, cooperated with one another to maintain our defense on the front lines. But as we multiplied into hundreds and even thousands, our memories grew faint."

I hardly remember the time when the original Emil was human. I've just heard from the other Emils that he had existed in a different body. But the other Emil that told me that didn't know about this place.

The original memories were scattered amongst us.

"The original Emil liked this place."

This was where everything that was important to him existed. He re-created his friend's cottage, planted flowers that were dear to his beloved, and relived his memories of the past...

"There were tough times and sad times, but memories of that journey were really treasured by the original."

I didn't experience it myself, but his memories—though faint and almost nonexistent now—live inside me now.

"And that original, where is he now?"

"I don't know. There were too many of us to keep track."

"I see..."

There were thousands and even tens of thousands of us, but most of us died in battle in order to protect the world that the original Emil had cherished and lived in with his friends.

"Thank you very much. Because of you I was able to remember something very important to me."

I was scared to remember before, but now I'm glad I remember.

"If I have this memory, I'll be able endure alone."

Even if I'm alone, I'll keep fighting my own battles. As long as I have this memory. That's what I think.

[Day Thirty-Three]

I spend the day after meeting Ms. 2B and Mr. 9S, and the day after that, just holed up in my home. I have some things I need to think through, alone.

After that, I spend some time running around the City Ruins and waiting for customers to arrive. But unfortunately, no one comes. Not even Ms. 2B and Mr. 9S.

I go to the shopping center too, but the two aren't there.

A few days ago, I heard there was a big battle in the Flooded City. I hope nothing happened to them—no, I'm probably worrying too much. I haven't known them long, but even during that short time I could see that they were growing ever stronger.

Maybe they moved far away. I want them to come visit me one time. I want to say goodbye...

[Day Fifty-Four]

Today, for the first time in a while, I run into Ms. 2B and Mr. 9S. I want to call out to them, but they are in battle, so I stop myself.

There are a few small types, and two four-legged types. There are a lot of enemies, but the two of them are fighting without a problem. If I helped I would probably be deadweight. That's how magnificently they are fighting.

I leave that area and cross the bridge. I want to see the lunar tear one last time.

A flower that's said to grant you any wish. Would it grant me mine?

To be honest, that myth sounds a bit suspicious. Because the original Emil grew as many lunar tears as he could, but he couldn't cure his little sister's disease.

And as I expected, that other person, who received the hair ornament made of lunar tears, her wish was—no, that's just what I, or the person I used to be, thought.

There was no way my wish was going to be granted. I knew that. On the other hand, I didn't expect anything. I knew it wasn't going to work, but I wanted to make a wish too.

"Emil!"

Ms. 2B calls to me, and I turn around. Apparently the two of them had finished off the horde of enemies. There isn't even a single scratch on either of them.

"You've gotten strong."

I have no intention of boasting that it was because of my weapons. Even without my weapons, these two would still be strong.

"You don't need my help anymore, right?"

"What do you mean?"

"No, it's nothing."

I'm glad I've run into them here. This way I can properly say my goodbyes.

"All the best."

I quickly leave the area. I need to hurry. I need to stop them before it's too late.

■   ■■

My responsibility in that battle was support from the rear. I carried supplies and replenished the Emils that were fighting on the front lines. I was running back and forth the whole time.

My body was this size so I would be able to nimbly run across the battlefield, and I had this form because I specialized in transporting supplies.

We were assigned sizes and bodies based on our responsibilities. The Emils on the front lines had high attack power, while the Emils that held up the solid defense were equipped with hard exoskeletons.

The original Emil apparently believed that diversity was the key to beat an enemy that fought with numbers. Just like how humans diversified their lifestyles and cultures to survive for so long.

Every day, I ran alone. From the Flooded City to that beach, day after day, I carried supplies. I brought recovery materials for my injured friends, and replenishment materials for my friends that used up all their magic.

They became less and less talkative as the days passed. We had always encouraged each other and fought together. But I noticed that conversation had started to disappear right around the time our numbers decreased drastically.

At the same time, my memories started to fade. Apparently exchanging old parts for new parts diluted memories. Which meant the fewer parts of original Emil I had, the fewer memories of the past I had.

I didn't have a hard exoskeleton like the attack-specialized Emils. I was pretty small and light. If an enemy missile landed near me, the shock wave was enough to send me flying. Since I was always running around the battlefield delivering supplies, I was always covered in scratches. And as a result, I had to exchange parts every day, and every time my memories of the original faded bit by bit.

But there was a silver lining. His memories had restricted me in a way. Those memories were of the original Emil, and not my own. Even if I had them, they were fake.

One by one, as the memories faded, somewhere in my mind I felt relief. Eventually I learned how to contain my emotions. I ran from my memories of struggle and sadness.

At that point all our defenses had crumbled. No matter how often we cloned ourselves, the number of enemies increased at a faster rate. The aliens mass-produced Machines, and bolstered their forces. Just like us, they were made to be adapt to any situation.

But the aliens didn't end up victorious. Tons of androids came down to Earth and took the edge in the battle against the aliens. Of course it wasn't easy. They seemed to have struggled as well…

Once my friends and I were scattered, we lost the majority of the original Emil's memories. We lived in the City Ruins, running shops for the androids. It was strange—our bodies still remembered that we had to deliver goods.

I would probably still be running around the City Ruins, unaware of who I am, if I hadn't met Ms. 2B and Mr. 9S, who helped me get my memories back…without realizing that my old friends were in danger.

I've been hearing their cries for help for a while now, but I had no idea what they meant. All I knew is that I heard strange noises in the desert, and that I was scared of them.

I need to go quickly. To where everyone is.

I use the teleportation magic that I remembered recently. The cluster of collapsing buildings disappear, and I am suddenly in the desert. And looking up I can see giant spheres in the air. They are attack-specialized Emils.

It brings back memories of days when I used to deliver them supplies. Everyone was so nice. They were always worn-out, but still had the patience to give me words of gratitude like "Thank you" and "Good work."

We all fought together during desperate times. The Emils on the battlefield really cared for each other. They were like family. I was a teeny bit envious of that. Supporting models like me, who worked from behind the front lines, rarely saw each other, and usually operated alone.

But on the other hand, caring for each other must've made it hard to lose friends one after the other. The fact that they were like family must've made it harder to watch the dying breaths of their friends.

"Everyone…"

It seems they don't remember me. Their groaning sounds like a wild animal's. They are Emils that lost their minds.

"1t hurts, 1t hurts," they say. I can hear cries for help too. "Etern1ty, 1t hurts… hurts…"

It's been thousands of years since the alien ambush. The whole time these Emils have been fighting on the front lines. A mind-bogglingly long time.

"Why…us…"

An infinite amount of self-cloning. Which meant that they lost an infinite number of friends.

"I'm…I'm g01ng t0 destr0y everyth1ng!"

"No you can't!"

"Th1s world… 1t's useless!"

"Stop! Don't do it!"

But my voice doesn't reach them. I don't have words to persuade them. No matter what I say, their suffering won't end…I know that.

"Everyone stop!"

I am instantly repulsed by their attack. I stand no chance, when they have power that could compete with aliens. But I have to stop them.

I face them many times. But every time I am batted away. My body is bent, and loses its tires…I end up sideways on the sand, unable to move.

"Emil!"

I hear Ms. 2B's voice.

"Are you okay?"

I see a worried Mr. 9S staring into my face. They probably noticed I was acting strangely and followed me here.

"Emil, what is that?"

"Those are…the products of my cloning. After several iterations of cloning and years of battle, they've lost their minds…"

My friends have great power but no sanity. There is no way I am going to let them be.

"I need to…put an end to this."

"It's okay! You should rest, Emil!"

The two of them leave me there and go to face the giant Emils. I don't have the strength to stop them anymore. Eventually my hearing fades and I am on the verge of losing consciousness. *I wonder if this is what dying feels like*, I think aimlessly.

I can hear voices. The voices of my friends.

"We did our best. On rainy days, windy days, and stormy days."

La la la, la la la, I hear singing.

"We kept fighting, even when our friends died."

I gradually start to remember what the later, quieter Emils were like. They kept their mouths shut, because as soon as they started talking nothing but pent-up resentment would come out, and only worsened their situation…

"But this eternal war, this eternal pain, this eternal struggle, it screams at us! That there's nothing in this world worth protecting! That this world has no meaning! That's what we hear!"

A piercing laugh echoes around us. "Warning: Large amounts of incoming magic," I hear Pod say.

"You…do you! Know! This pain! This sadness! This despair! Can you feel it?"

It is clear what they are going to do—release a giant amount of magic in one immense explosion and self-destruct, taking this cruel world along for the ride.

World? What about the world? What about this cruel world?

I suddenly remember someone's voice. It was a cold and blunt voice, but kind—that person's voice was very similar to Ms. 2B's. I hear a calculated voice of a wise man too. A kind and mellow voice as well.

The original Emil's memories are starting to resurface. His treasured memories. Memories of that journey.

"Still, this is wrong!" I scream. Even if my friends had lost their sanity, the very same memories must be buried deep inside them.

"No matter how much pain or agony that person had, he never gave up. She fought believing that one day she would overcome all of that! You have to keep going, even if it's in vain! Isn't that right, Kainé?"

I can't attack or defend for my life, but I have to do this. I can't give up.

"This is the world that person tried to protect!"

I feel my friends come to. Our memories are scattered, and faded, but there's still some traces of…that person.

I gather all the magic within me to stop my friends from self-destructing. So I can make an effort until the very end.

It's quiet. I only hear the sound of wind. It seems I'm still alive.

"I'm no…good. I remembered something that important at the… very last second."

They are fake memories, but the pain of losing someone dear to me is real. I was running away from that this whole time. I tried to shut away my memories and forget them. But that made me forget things I wasn't supposed to forget.

I can't hear my friends anymore. It seems I was able to stop the explosion. Ms. 2B and Mr. 9S probably lent a hand as well.

"Ms. 2B and Mr. 9S… yu helped me until the very end…"

I see Ms. 2B shake her head in silence. Mr. 9S tells me, "You'll get better if we fix you up." They're very kind people.

They lived through harsh and cruel battles almost every day. But you couldn't tell. Why were people that lived through terrible battles so kind? That's right, that person was kind too…

I can feel my consciousness slowly fading. My memories—or rather, memories that weren't mine—gradually disappear.

It's okay. This is fine. I am about to let everything go.

"Emil," I hear a voice call out. It isn't Ms. 2B or Mr. 9S, but a nostalgic voice. I look up in surprise. This was, this was…

Though my vision is hazy, I see a smiling person waving their hand. A floating book as well.

I see him…I actually see him again. The lunar tears have actually granted me my wish.

"Welcome back, Emil. Good work."

I stand up, and head toward the person I yearned to see the most. All the while repeating the name I loved to say.

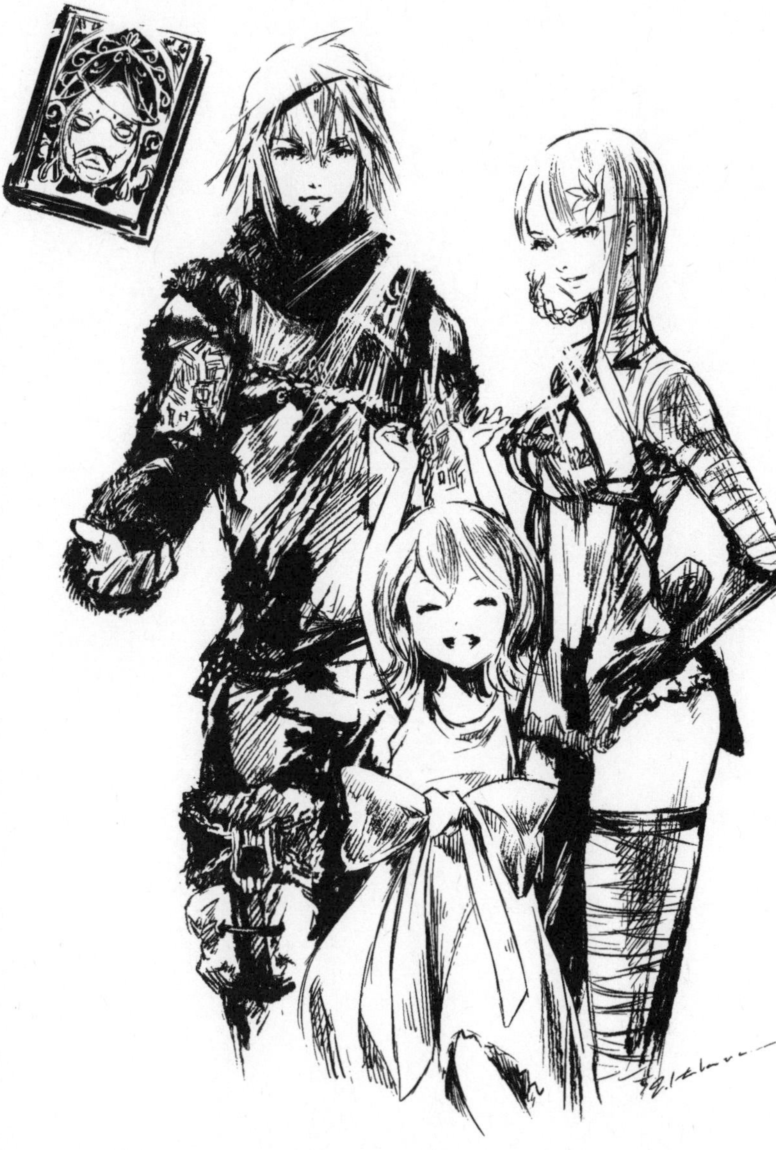

AUTHOR BIOS

JUN EISHIMA was born in 1964, in Fukuoka Prefecture, Japan. Work includes <u>Drag-On Dragoon 3 Story Side</u>, <u>FINAL FANTASY XIII Episode Zero</u>, and <u>FINAL FANTASY XIII-2 Fragment Before</u> (Square Enix). Under the name Emi Nagashima has also authored <u>The Cat Thief Hinako's Case Files: Your lover will be confiscated</u> (Tokuma Bunko) and other titles. In 2016, received the 69th Mystery Writers of Japan Award (Short Story division) for the title <u>Old Maid</u>.

■ ■■

YOKO TARO is the game director for the <u>NieR</u> and <u>Drakengard</u> series.